P
BOHONIS

Margaret McFarland

A <u>73 WINDSOR</u> NOVEL

3rd Season Publications
www.3rdseason.ca

Margaret McFarland
© 2018, Phyllis Bohonis

Designed by Crowe Creations
Cover design © 2018 Crowe Creations
Author photo © 2014 Sue Quinn

ISBN: 978-1-9994378-0-0

To my good friend Dianne.

Hope you enjoy an evening with "Margaret".

[signature]

To all the dedicated volunteers working in
missions around the world.

Grow old along with me!
 The best is yet to be.
                    — Robert Browning

73 Windsor: Margaret McFarland

Chapter One

"So you have a man in your life?" Sarah looked flabbergasted.

"And you haven't told us about him? What kind of friend are you?" Olivia tried to look upset but the gleam in her eye said something entirely different.

"He must be a real hunk and she's hiding him." Helen joined the chorus.

Margaret looked around the bridge table. All eyes were on her. "Well, I wouldn't say he's a hunk, exactly."

"Yeah. Yeah. He has a great personality and an even greater sense of humour." Sarah smiled as she folded her cards and set them aside. "Come on, give us the nitty gritty. All of it."

Helen placed her hand on Margaret's wrist. "Start at the beginning."

"I know you've all been bored to death with my seemingly never-ending list of ailments. You told me all I needed was a man in my life."

"So you went out and got one. Way to go, Margaret!"

"Sarah, let her finish."

"Yes." Olivia agreed. "Let her finish. I want to hear about the good stuff."

"All I'll say is you were right. Since I met Clarke I've not had a thing to complain about. I've never felt healthier."

She was positively beaming. The three women didn't take their eyes from her. She didn't care. Let them wait. Whether she and Clarke were sleeping together or not was no one's business. In the meantime, she would have some fun with her friends. Not mischievous by nature, she felt they deserved a little teasing. It was Olivia that had told Margaret the only thing that would get rid of her hypochondria was to get laid. After years of playing bridge every Thursday afternoon, they were more sisters than friends. She knew they'd had some good-natured fun at her expense. It was time to turn the tables.

"Clarke and I met about seven weeks ago. He started a conversation and I can't tell you how happy I am that he did. It didn't take long to realize we have a lot in common. He's definitely not a hunk. In fact, he's rather … not. Deceiving as that is, he's the best thing that's happened to me in a long time. Girls, I can guarantee you I won't be having any more stomach problems."

"Does Clarke, the superman, have a last name?" Olivia was standing, leaning against the kitchen doorway with her arms crossed in front of her.

"Ingram."

"Does he work?"

"No. He's retired."

Helen's eyes hadn't left Margaret's face.

"Do you have a question, Helen?"

"When are we going to meet Clarke Ingram?"

"Soon. He's visiting his grandchildren in southern Ontario for a few weeks."

"A few weeks? Are you going to survive without him for that long?"

"Don't worry, Sarah. He took very good care of me before he left." Margaret's wistful smile only added to their startled expressions. Finally, she shook her head and stood. "It looks like we're not playing any more bridge, so I'll bring the cheesecake and coffee."

"You can't just leave us hanging, Margaret. That's not fair. We need details."

"Sorry, girls. That's all you're getting."

Chapter Two

Margaret smiled as she closed the door after the last of her friends left. *I wish I could be a fly on the wall in Sarah's condo. The three of them will be just hopping off the floor trying to figure out who Clarke is and how I've managed to keep him a secret. Let them wonder for a little while longer.* She didn't want to hurt their feelings but right now she wanted to keep her relationship with Clarke private. It's not that her friends wouldn't be supportive of her happiness, or that they'd cross the privacy line, it's just … well, it is what it is. For now.

The fact that she'd stretched the truth a little was another reason to keep the relationship off limits for a while. She was feeling much better and Clarke was indeed responsible. That much was true. *If only I'd met him years ago.*

Helen Mercier had been Helen Whittaker before she married Gerald a few months earlier. If she could start all over with the love of a new man at her age, then why should the other girls be so flabbergasted that Margaret might do the same thing? She was being unfair, she knew. They would want her to be just as happy as Helen. The only thing was, Clarke was different from Gerald. Was she worried they might not accept him? Were virile good looks, a.k.a. hunkiness, that important? Sooner or later, she'd find out.

Later, when the dishes were done and the kitchen and dining room cleaned, she would call Clarke. What a nice feeling it was to have someone with whom she could share her daily experiences.

When she and Hugh were newlyweds, they had put off having a family so they could enjoy some time experiencing married life without the responsibility of raising children. When they finally became comfortable with the idea of a baby in their lives and after years of trying unsuccessfully, followed by the heartbreak of failed attempts through fertility clinics, they realized the decision had been taken out of their hands. They had discussed adoption, but Hugh had not been sure he could truly love a child who was not his own. They had settled into their careers, travelling locally and enjoying the freedom that childless couples experience. They didn't have any pets, anything that might interfere with their personal freedom. They both worked close to the downtown core and would meet for dinner out two or three nights a week.

After several years they had bought a summer cottage on White Lake where they spent many of their weekends. Hugh had never been a great long-distance traveller. He much preferred short jaunts to nearby places so this suited his lifestyle. Soon they gave up their city house and purchased a condominium on Windsor Street in downtown Ottawa so that only one yard required maintenance and they could also spend time away without worry of break-ins or vandalism. Usually on long week-ends over the summer months, one or another of their siblings would visit, nephews and nieces enjoying the water and beach activities. As the children became teenagers with city friends with whom they preferred to spend weekends, the cottage became a tranquil retreat for Margaret and Hugh, a place to enjoy quiet walks, canoeing and kayaking.

When retirement was offered to Hugh at the age of fifty-five, he accepted it. Margaret's retirement with a decent pension wouldn't come until she was sixty. Just months before her scheduled retirement, Hugh had a massive heart attack on the golf course and was pronounced dead at the scene.

Margaret was devastated. Hugh had been her whole life. Her

brother, Casey, and his wife, Elaine, had been supportive for a short while but soon became caught up in their own lives again. She couldn't blame them. She knew she wasn't much fun to be around. Her group of bridge friends who lived in the same condo building were her biggest support system. Without them, she didn't know how she would have survived. Helen was married. Olivia had never married — the one and only love of her life had died early in their relationship and she had never found another to take his place. Sarah had been married several times before she decided she liked being single better.

The four of them had helped each other through countless tragedies, big and small, over the years. This past year had been sheer hell for Helen but the happiness she found at the end of it had been a true fairy tale ending. Now it was Margaret's time. Clarke was the leprechaun sitting on the pot of gold at the end of her rainbow. That rainbow was shining brighter every day.

When she had learned he was a retired Presbyterian minister and had spent a lot of time working for foreign missions, she'd been full of questions. Where had he travelled? What was it like working in third world countries? What had been the attraction that took him on his first mission? Had his wife gone with him? She found his life story so fascinating. When it became more and more difficult for him to travel, his daughter and her husband picked up where he had left off. They had spent a few weeks during each of the past three years helping spread the word of God and assisting with the well-being of those living in need in the jungles of Peru. Clarke was always glad to stay with his grandchildren during these times.

The phone interrupted her thoughts.

"Hello."

"Hi, sweetheart. How did the afternoon go?"

"I was just about to call you, Clarke. The afternoon was the usual gossip and tidbits of news until I dropped my bomb. To put it mildly, my friends were surprised, pleasantly I think, to learn I have a man in my life."

"They didn't mind that the man is a mean old tyrant who's threatening to remove you from their lives? You did tell them that I want to sweep you away and keep you all to myself, didn't you?"

She giggled. "I thought I'd save that for the next session. I did let them know how extremely happy I am."

"Just as I am, Maggie. I miss you already. When is your next card game?"

His casual use of her name always brought a smile to her face. "Not for two weeks."

"Good. That will give you lots of time to come and meet my family. I don't know why I didn't bring you with me."

"Yes, you do. You needed time to tell your daughter about me. Us."

"I told her all about us before I came. Kirsten's happy for me. She would like to meet you. Will you come?"

"Clarke, everything is happening so fast. We've only known each other a few weeks. Besides, she and her husband are away."

"If you have nothing pressing you can stay until they return. You can help me with the grandchildren."

Grandchildren. The word filled her with warmth. She hadn't given a thought to Clarke being a grandfather. Had never given a thought to becoming even a pseudo-grandmother.

"You said they're close in age? Ten and nine years old? My goodness, I haven't had much experience with children."

"You don't need experience. They practically take care of themselves and they don't believe that their old grandfather has a girlfriend. A beautiful one at that. You have to come to show them I'm telling the truth or I'll owe them a trip to Canada's Wonderland."

Margaret moved to the mirror in the foyer and sucked in her

breath. Holding it all in didn't help the slight roll just above her expanding waistline. And she could suck in her breath all day and all night and it wouldn't help the dimples in her backside and thighs. But Clarke thought she was beautiful. She could admit to having a pretty face but as she looked in the mirror, everything south of her chin was, well … heading farther south.

"Maggie, are you there?"

"Uh, yes. Clarke, I have some things I have to take care of. How will it be if I come down at the beginning of the week?"

"I guess I can put up with these two monsters by myself for a few more days." Margaret could hear giggling in the background.

"I'll book a seat for you on a flight into Hamilton. If you come on Sunday, the kids will be able to come with me to pick you up at the airport. We could all go out for Sunday dinner. Maybe we could take a couple of days for ourselves, just the two of us, after Kirsten and Mitchell return before we come home."

"I'll pay for my own flight, Clarke, and I'll see if I can get things done by Sunday." She smiled as she hung up the phone after promising to let him know soon if she could indeed travel on Sunday.

Men, they don't know what a woman has to do before travelling — especially when you have to live up to being thought beautiful.

She made a list. Her life seemed to consist of lists. First was the hair salon. Her roots needed "conditioning". Manicure, pedicure and waxing definitely were on the schedule. Plus some shopping was in order.

Chapter Three

"Helen, have you talked to Margaret this morning?" Olivia was in the hallway outside Helen's door.

"No. I called but she didn't answer."

"There was no answer when I called last night either." Olivia suggested a visit was in order.

The four women called each other every morning and every night. They weren't being nosy. They had almost lost a neighbour who hadn't even been missed prior to being found in some bushes in the area a few years earlier. She had lain there beaten and semi-conscious for two days. After that, they devised a system to keep in touch with each other for safety's sake. If one didn't answer after being called twice in a day, whoever had that person's key would check the apartment.

The two women went up to Margaret's condo and rang the bell. When Margaret didn't answer after three rings, Olivia put the key in the lock. It was obvious in a minute that the apartment was empty, but they found a note on the dining room table.

> Girls,
>
> I hope I didn't worry you. I figured you would come when I didn't answer the phone.
>
> I accepted an invitation to join Clarke at his daughter's home in Hamilton. It was a hasty

decision and I had to rush to catch a flight. I'll be in touch in a day or two once I'm settled.

Love, Margaret

"Damn that woman! Why won't she get a cell phone like everyone else? She could have texted us to let us know she was on her way or even that she had arrived and where she is. The note isn't even dated." Olivia had fire in her eyes.

"I spoke with her yesterday morning, but it was little more than a hi and good-bye. She must have left sometime yesterday if she didn't answer her phone last night. It's not like her not to say anything."

"It's that Clarke guy. I hope he's not one of those controllers. They separate women from their friends first, then their family, and before you know it, they've taken control of the poor soul's bank accounts and their lives."

"Let's not jump to conclusions, Olivia. He might be a really nice guy. She certainly seemed happy when she told us about him."

"She hardly knows the guy. When did she say she met him? Three weeks ago?"

"I think she said seven weeks ago."

"Helen, don't split hairs. We know nothing about him or where he's taken her. It's his daughter's home and we don't even know what her name is. You're right. It's not like Margaret to be so secretive. Damn. Damn. I'm buying her a cell phone so I can at least have the satisfaction of texting her and giving her hell when she pulls tricks like this."

"I don't think she has much experience with men. Hugh spoiled her rotten. He worshipped the ground she walked on and I wouldn't be surprised if she thinks all men are like him. Margaret can be so naïve. She's too trusting, Olivia."

"Let's go downstairs and talk about this over coffee with

Sarah. We have to figure out what we're going to do."

Sarah, of course, knew nothing more about Clarke or his family than the other two did. Beyond suggesting they call Casey, Margaret's brother, she couldn't offer any other advice. After more conversation, they decided not to worry her brother before they knew if there was anything to be worried about.

"Damn woman. Did she not give us a single thought of concern? She could be anywhere in the world. What if she needs us?" Olivia, the most independent one of the group was also the most concerned.

Helen stood and turned to the others. "Let's leave it for a few more days. They probably went off for a few romantic days together and she'll have so much to tell us about when she gets home — after we give her a piece of our individual minds."

"Clarke the Superman is supposed to be babysitting his grandchildren, isn't he? I don't see how that could be very romantic." Sarah rose and looked at Helen.

Helen thought for a moment then observed, "What if he needed help with one of the grandchildren and didn't want to upset his daughter. That might make for a quick response on Margaret's part. Or maybe his daughter is injured somewhere and he had to go to her and Margaret is staying with the little ones."

"We could speculate into next week about her sudden departure when it may be nothing at all. He may have just missed her and wanted her to come and she went. Simple as that. Let's wait and see. If we interfere, she may be as upset as all hell. She's a grown woman and we just have to trust her. It was inconsiderate of her but, hey, she's in love." Sarah raised her arms in a questioning shrug. "If any one of us hears from her, we'll let the others know."

They agreed on a do nothing for four days situation, then Sarah walked to the door and let the women out. She could hear their mumbling all the way down the hall.

Chapter Four

Margaret knew her friends would be upset, maybe even angry with her. The thought had kept her from enjoying her flight. The smaller airport in Hamilton made her arrival simple and allowed her a seamless entry into the waiting area.

"Is that her? The lady with the white hair over there?" A young voice reached Margaret's ears above the usual airport noises. She looked in the direction from which it seemed to come and sure enough, there were three grinning faces staring at her, one older and two about ten years old.

Margaret learned their names were Kelly and Sean and that Kelly was one year and seventeen minutes older than her brother. Clarke bussed her cheek with his lips while the children giggled. "Okay, kids, each of you take a bag and we'll get Mrs. McFarland into the car."

"Good thing she only has two bags, Grandpa, so you don't have to carry any."

"That's right, so my job will be to hang on to her so that she doesn't trip and fall." He placed his hand under Margaret's elbow and turned her toward the exit. The twins exchanged knowing glances before pulling the luggage out the door.

Once in the car, Clarke was reminded by his grandchildren that he had promised them supper at a restaurant. Since it was not a long ride between the airport and home, they decided to go to a Swiss Chalet where the kids would be sure to find something they like on the menu. During the meal Margaret learned that Kelly was in grade five and Sean was in grade four and that Sean played soccer and Kelly was into tennis. During the winter they both played hockey. When Sean called her Mrs. McFarland again, she gave them permission to call her Margaret.

"Margaret? I thought your name is Maggie."

Clarke interrupted by saying that her name really is Margaret but Maggie is a short term for it. "Maggie was what we called a favourite cousin of mine whose name was Margaret also. Some people even change it to Peggy. My cousin was pretty nice, for a girl, and since Mrs. McFarland is pretty nice too, I just naturally started calling her Maggie."

"Why would the name Margaret get changed to Peggy? They don't even sound the same." Kelly joined in.

Margaret answered by saying, "Some people pronounced Maggie as Meggie and then somehow it morphed into Peggy."

"Peggy. Peggy. Margaret. Maggie. Meggie. Peggy." Kelly kept rolling the names around in her mouth. She finally stopped when the waiter brought them fudge brownies with ice cream on top.

Kelly showed Margaret into the guest room which was on the lower of the bi-level home and was complete with its own en suite. The warmth of colours and the abundance of three windows gave the room a cheery atmosphere rather than the feeling of being in the basement. Margaret smiled when she ran her hand over the dressing table of a mid-twentieth century bedroom suite with its rounded corners, deep drawers on each side and an upholstered bench. The polished wood gave it a showroom finish which told the story of a tenderly cared for set of furniture. *It must have belonged to someone's grandparents.*

"My grandpa made me give it a good dusting today and Sean helped me make up the bed with fresh linen." The young girl turned the light on in the bathroom. "I remembered to put fresh towels and soap for you."

"Take your time to freshen up and get a second wind after two hours with the children. I'm sure they'll want to show you around the house and yard before it gets dark."

As Clarke spoke from the top of the stairs, Margaret could hear another voice chiming in. "Grandpa, can we show Mrs., I mean Margaret, around the house?" Sean's voice became louder as he descended.

"You just leave Maggie alone for a bit. She must be tired from her flight and putting up with you two monkeys for the last two hours. Give her a chance to unpack and get familiar with her room then she'll come up when she's ready."

Clarke urged Kelly to close the door on her way out.

Margaret looked at the time and realized it stayed lighter slightly longer in this part of the province. In Ottawa the shadows would have been covering the ground by now. She opened her bag and placed her clothing in the top drawer of the tallboy and took her toiletries into the en suite. She touched up her makeup and made her way up the stairs.

Clarke was right, the kids were waiting for her to see their bedrooms, each wanting to be first. Their rooms reflected their personalities. Sean's was decorated with sports figures on the walls in various poses of their chosen sports, a basket was attached to the outside of the closet door and ball sat on a chair. She saw an open duffle bag on the floor with a soccer ball inside.

Kelly's would be painted lilac or pink she thought. However, when she stepped inside the door she was confronted by a huge grey elephant. Looking around, there were murals of almost life-size jungle animals on every one of the soft green walls. A rope hung from the ceiling in a corner with stuffed monkeys posed in various positions along the length of it. A few painted jungle trees and tall grass filled some of the wall spaces not occupied by animals. On closer inspection, she could just make out a lioness on one wall hiding amid the grass.

"I'm going to work in Africa when I'm older." Spoken with a casual air of finality, Kelly beamed as Margaret looked around her room. The older woman realized that the young girl would grow into a special breed of woman, not one to spend her days in dresses and high heels then face the stress of commutes to and from an office. Not a concrete jungle for this lady, she would settle for nothing less than the real thing.

"I'm sure you will, dear. I'm sure you will." Margaret felt a spark of envy that this determined young individual, not yet in her puberty, was so certain how her life would play out.

"My friend Justin's sister has unicorns in her bedroom and what does my sister have? A jungle." Sean was not in the least scornful that his sister didn't have fluff and frill in her room. He seemed equally as proud of her choices as she was.

Chapter Five

After the children were in bed, Clarke mixed drinks for Margaret and himself while she made herself comfortable on the back deck and watched the reflection of the stars dancing in the swimming pool. Sometimes she missed the solitude of a back yard at the end of a summer's day where one could relax and enjoy the fragrance of the flower gardens with the hint of chlorine in the mix. Even the sometimes-irritable sounds of crickets were a welcome memory of days gone by.

Another sound, one of glasses clinking on a tray, made her turn to slide the door open for Clarke. He could manage most things quite well but when his hands were occupied, he had to rely totally on his own balance and there were times when it let him down. She took the tray from him so he could hold on to the door frame as he passed through. He had lost his left leg from above the knee in an accident he was reluctant to discuss. Reliant on a prosthesis, he managed to live a normal life and did most things persons with two healthy legs would do. He used two canes a good part of the time but at home he often removed his prosthesis and got around by wheelchair. Kirsten and Mitchell had added some features to their house to make it completely wheelchair accessible for Clarke.

He settled his lean frame into a deck chair beside Margaret. "Well? Do you think you can take the noise and interruptions of the children for a few days?"

"They are lovely children, Clarke. Their parents have done an excellent job with their manners. I quite like them."

Pride showed in his face. "They seem to do well in school and are active in sports so I guess they're getting a pretty well-rounded education. Sunday service is attended by all of them even if it means missing a sporting event. I don't hear them complain too much so they must accept it as a way of life. Kirsten and Stephen are both passionate about the children's developing a strong foundation in faith."

He sipped his drink and turned to Margaret. "I wasn't sure how you would take to the children after not having any of your own."

"This is a test then?" A mischievous gleam filled her eyes. "If I pass the 'grandchildren test' I'm on the possibility list?"

His eyes were more serious. "Maggie, when a married woman has no children of her own, there are many possible reasons why. Perhaps she has no patience for them. Maybe she has no confidence in her ability to actually care for them. Maybe she is unable to conceive or carry, which can be emotionally and/or physically devastating. Maybe she has lost a child and couldn't bear going through that experience again. Or maybe these same scenarios belonged to her husband and she loved him enough to accept them. Or maybe it's another of the hundreds of other reasons why not.

"It's not my business, but I did feel concern that my grand-children might not have a place in your life — for whatever reason. I knew the instant I met you that you were a woman I wanted to know better. I wanted to hear you laugh, to smile, maybe even to sing. You had some quality in you that stirred emotion in me. As I got to know you, I realized I couldn't wait to see you each time. I've grown very fond of you. My daughter, her husband and my grandchildren are a very big part of my life. I hoped and prayed they might become a part of yours. I thought the only way to know if this is possible is by jumping in with both feet."

He paused and looked down at his own foot and his prosthetic one beside it. "Well, with one foot anyway."

She was relieved to see him smile as he said it. "Did you take the *children's* acceptance of a pseudo-grandmother into this scenario as well? They may not appreciate a strange lady coming on the scene and pretending to be their new granny."

He took her hand in his. "I knew that wouldn't be a problem. I've done nothing more these past two weeks than talk about you. They believe you are their fairy godmother who has come to rescue their poor old granddad from a life of loneliness. They already knew, as did I, that they couldn't help but fall in love with you … as did I." He kissed the palm of her hand. "Sean has already asked why we have to leave when his parents come home. He wants both of us, although I do think it's mainly you, to stay longer."

He turned her face with his other hand until their faces were scant inches apart. "Besides you're not their new granny. You're my beautiful girlfriend, remember?"

He leaned in and kissed her gently but lingeringly on her lips. "Aren't you?"

Margaret's eyes remained closed for a few seconds. When she opened them she searched his eyes, his face, then smiled. Then started laughing.

"Maggie, I'm being very serious here. I thought I was creating a romantic scene on a beautiful patio fragrant with flowers, under a moonlit sky with stars dancing around … and all you can do is laugh?"

Margaret stood and walked to the far end of the pool. She looked up at the sky, then at the hydrangeas, anything for time to compose herself. Finally, she walked back to her chair and took both of Clarke's hands in hers.

"I am so sorry, Clarke. My rudeness is unforgivable." She raised his hands to her lips and caressed the backs of both with delicate kisses.

"I couldn't help but in a moment of, I don't know, panic maybe, compare that you were concerned about my acceptance of your adorable grandchildren when I have been wondering how you are going to feel about my overly protective but loving, dearest friends. They have been my only family for a number of years now. We are closer than sisters. In fact, I can just imagine what is going on at 73 Windsor Street since I left in such a hurry to be with a man they have not even met. That is why I was laughing. You have no idea how protective we all can be of each other." She thought back to the time they foolishly thought Helen was being taken advantage of by Gerald. That poor man had been a victim of their full wrath.

"They can't be that bad."

She gave him one of her "oh really" looks but controlled her laughter this time.

"Can they?"

Chapter Six

"Peggy? Peggy, are you awake?

Margaret looked at the clock radio and saw it was 8:30 in the morning. *Peggy? Who? What?* Then she realized it was Kelly tapping softly on her door.

"Come in, dear."

Kelly, still in pj's peeked in then closed the door as she slipped through and sat on the foot of Margaret's bed.

"Did you have a good sleep?"

"Yes, I did, Kelly. Thank you for coming to ask. Am I the last to wake up?"

Kelly giggled. "Yes, but that's okay. Grandpa said that's why you are so beautiful, because you make sure you get your beauty sleep."

Margaret didn't quite know how to respond so she reached for her housecoat instead.

"Is that *really* why you are beautiful?" Kelly scrutinized the older woman's face.

"I don't know that sleep has as much to do with how you look as genes do."

"Jeans? Why would jeans make your face look different?"

"Well, because ... Oh, you think I'm talking about blue jeans. Pants."

"Aren't you?"

Margaret worked to keep from smiling and possibly embarrassing the girl. "No. I'm talking about the kind of genes,

20

spelled g-e-n-e-s, that are cells, part of your body, things you inherit from your parents and grandparents. It's called your genetic make-up — and not the kind of make-up that you put on your face from a bottle."

"You mean the reason some people look like their mothers and others look like their dads?"

"Exactly. You are very perceptive. No matter how much sleep you get you can't change how you look. Well, that's not exactly true, lack of sleep can make you look tired. If you continually miss a lot of sleep, you can look haggard, which is rather unpleasant." Not wanting to contradict Clarke, she quickly added. "That's why some women say they want to sleep in, because they need their beauty sleep."

"Grandpa always says silly things trying to make excuses for people. Why didn't he just say you were sleeping in?"

"Maybe he was afraid you'd think I was just plain lazy. Is that bacon I smell?"

"Yes. Grandpa is making bacon and pancakes. I wanted to tell you because he has a rule. He always makes the last one to the table load the dishwasher. Sean is outside playing so you can still beat him if you hurry." She headed for the door. "Don't worry, my mom wears her housecoat for breakfast all the time."

Margaret quickly turned the shower on and covered her hair with a plastic cap. It took only a few minutes to towel herself dry and apply body lotion and face cream. A touch of mascara and a brush of blush to match her pink and violet sundress and she was on her way to the kitchen. Sean was just coming in through the garage door and seemed hell bent on reaching his chair before she did. However, a cough from his grandfather stopped him in his tracks and a nod of Clarke's head had the boy reaching to hold Margaret's chair for her. Before her bum touched the seat, she backed out, mentioned forgetting something and went back downstairs. When she returned Sean was in his seat and Clarke held her chair.

"Peggy, now you'll have to load the dishwasher. You should have sat when Sean held your chair for you. Did you forget?"

"Oh my, I did forget but I needed a tissue in my pocket." She winked at Sean who smiled smugly as he reached for a pancake.

"Since I think there might have been some collusion going on here, we will all clear the table, wipe everything down including the stove and sweep the floor. And that includes you, Maggie." Clarke tried to sound parental and used what must have been his pulpit voice.

"Now, who's up to a trip to the Royal Botanical Gardens?"

A chorus of "me's" went up including one from Margaret.

"Peggy, can I sit beside you at lunch?" A wistful smile played across Kelly's face.

Chapter Seven

Days of sightseeing followed, including a day trip to Niagara Falls. They even drove to Toronto for a Blue Jays afternoon game against the Yankees. It went into extra innings, but the Jays came out victorious. They had a wiener roast one night in the fire pit built into one end of the patio, with a few of the children's friends invited for a swim party.

It was during the wiener roast that Margaret remembered she had not talked to her friends. With amazing quickness, she stood and almost ran into the kitchen. Clarke noticed her frenzied look and followed her inside. "What is it, Maggie?"

She started to laugh then stopped. "Clarke, I've been having such a great time, I forgot to call my friends. They must be frantic with worry."

He smiled. "Well, we mustn't let your sisters get upset. You can take the phone from here into your room or the living room and talk privately away from all this noise."

Margaret walked into the living room saying over her shoulder, "Believe me, they're already upset, there's no doubt about that."

Margaret decided to try Helen first. She was usually the calmest and most level-headed one. There was no answer. Next on the list was Sarah.

"Is this you, Margaret McFarland?"

"Maybe I should hang up and try Olivia."

"You're lucky I answered. I didn't recognize the number

displayed or the name."

"I'm sorry. For everything."

"As you should be!"

"I should have called sooner, I know, but I've been so busy and having such a good time, I just ... forgot." She realized how lame that sounded. There was silence on the other end of the line. "Okay, so that's how it's going to be."

Sarah sighed, and Margaret knew her friend wasn't going to let her off the hook easily.

"I am truly sorry, Sarah, to all of you. I got caught up in the excitement and should have been more thoughtful about your concerns. There is absolutely no reason for you to worry but you would have no way of knowing that."

"No, we don't even know where you are, for heaven's sake."

"I know. I know. It was plain foolish of me to leave with no information about where I'd be. I forget that you girls keep in touch by cell phone and, well, I just plain don't have nor want one. I didn't know the phone number or even the address here because Clarke always calls me from his own cell phone. Sarah, what's that pinging noise I hear?"

"If I lose you it's because I'm getting on the elevator but you damn well better call back. I'm taking this call to Olivia's so you can tell us both all about the hijinks you're up to. I'll put it on speaker phone."

About thirty-five minutes into the call, Margaret was interrupted by Kelly calling frantically from outside. "Peggy, Peggy! We have to call 911. Grandpa fell in the swimming pool and is drowning."

Chapter Eight

Margaret had the foresight to grab Clarke's cell phone before getting into the car to follow the ambulance to the hospital. He was unconscious, but his heart was beating when they closed the doors on the vehicle and drove away, lights flashing and siren blaring.

After changing quickly into dry clothes and ushering Clarke's grandchildren into the car, she had left the house and young swim party guests in the care of the parents who lived the closest. She knew no one and had to trust the neighbours who had offered to shut everything down and get the other children safely home. They had also offered to take Kelly and Sean home with them, but Margaret knew the children would rather remain with her and be close to their grandfather.

Everything had happened so quickly. A child who couldn't swim had accidentally been knocked into the water. Clarke had quickly rolled his wheelchair to the edge of the pool in an attempt to throw the child a line but in adjusting his weight the chair had toppled into the water trapping him underneath it. The struggling child had somehow managed to get out of the water, but no one could lift the chair off Clarke. When Kelly came running in, Margaret dialled 911, handed the phone to Kelly to talk to the operator, then she jumped into the pool and successfully freed Clarke. His lungs were already full of water. She tried to resuscitate him, but he was still unconscious when the paramedics arrived.

In the meantime, neighbours whose son was among the children at the little party heard all the commotion and came over to see what was going on. Thank goodness they had. It freed Margaret to change her clothes and get the children and her to the hospital. At the last minute, she remembered Clarke's phone with which she would be able to reach Kirsten once she got to the hospital and knew what kind of news she would give to the poor woman about her dad.

Kelly and Sean were uncharacteristically quiet in the backseat of the car. The poor, poor children. What must be running through their minds? Even though she had been with them twenty-four hours a day for almost a week, she was still a relative stranger to them. And here they were riding in their grandfather's car to the hospital, not knowing if he were still alive, and their parents were thousands of miles away in a foreign country. They needed the comforting embrace of someone they knew. Someone who loved them and they loved back. There were no aunts or uncles around, at least not on their mother's side. She wasn't sure about Mitchell's, but none had been mentioned. She would ask the children once they knew how Clarke was.

The blocks to the hospital seemed like miles. Finally, she was down the escarpment and turning into the parking spaces by the hospital emergency. The children each reached for one of her hands. They were trembling. Shock? Possibly. Poor kids. She should have asked one of the neighbours to come with them, or even drive them but the other children at the house had needed taking care of. They probably were in shock also. A fun evening had turned to terror in the blink of an eye. No, Kelly and Sean were her responsibility and she was happy she was there for them … and for Clarke. They were finally in the triage area of the emergency and someone had gone to locate Clarke. They had been less than a half hour behind the ambulance.

A nurse guided them to a waiting room and they were told

someone would come to talk with them shortly. When Margaret asked about his situation, she was told he had weak but stable vitals when he arrived but had not gained consciousness as far as the nurse knew. He was going through various testing procedures at the moment.

Margaret sat on a leather sofa with the children clinging to each of her arms. She worked them free and wrapped them around the children's shoulders pulling their trembling bodies in close. How could she make them stop shaking? What words of comfort could she give ten-year-old and nine-year-old children that wouldn't frighten them even more?

"I know you both have been taught how to pray. I think your grandpa would like it if we all prayed for him now. Do you know the Lord's prayer?"

They nodded, lowered their heads and joined hands, saying together. "Our Father, who art in heaven …"

When they had finished, Kelly turned to Margaret. "Do you think Grandpa has gone to heaven?"

"I think the doctor would have come out and told us if that were so. They are most likely working very hard making sure he stays with us for a long time yet. That's why we have to pray — to make sure God helps the doctors do everything they can to make him well again."

She could feel Sean's sobs before she heard them. "Do Mommy and Daddy know?"

"We'll call them as soon as the doctor comes and tells us your grandpa is okay. No sense in worrying your parents for nothing."

No sooner were the words out of her mouth, when two uniformed police officers approached the visitors lounge. The older of the two started toward her.

"You're the person waiting for Mr. Ingram to be examined?"

It took an hour to fill the police in on what had happened at the pool. They needed to know the complete sequence of events from the time Margaret went inside to talk on the phone until the paramedics arrived. The children filled in all the details after Margaret had left and until Kelly came running in crying for help. She had to give them all her personal information. They examined her driver's licence and asked repeated questions about her relationship with Clarke. They asked numerous questions of the children about their parents' reasons for being away, the time frame, and their relationship to Margaret. It was routine questioning after an accident of this type occurs, they explained. The possibility of foul play had to be excluded and that the children were not victims of any wrongdoing or negligence.

Margaret was able to tell them the name of the church-based agency under whose umbrella Kirsten and Mitchell were working. It wasn't until after they left that she remembered their number was in Clarke's phone. Everything was so nerve racking, she couldn't think of everything. She hoped the police wouldn't catch up with Kirsten anyway until after they knew how her dad was.

When a half hour had passed and no word was forthcoming, Margaret felt uneasy about not calling Clarke's daughter. After another fifteen minutes, she sought out one of the nurses to see what was happening. "He's gone for a CT scan. It will help them determine any trauma to the brain. He won't be gone long. Are you his wife?"

"No. No, I'm not. I am his close friend and I'm with his grandchildren. His daughter is out of the country and I want to call her, but I don't know what to tell her."

It was after midnight and the children should have been taken home to bed, but she didn't want to leave. She didn't want Clarke to think he was alone if he woke up. She decided to make the call hoping it wasn't past bed time in Peru. Kirsten had a right to know her dad was in the hospital in a coma. She also hoped Kirsten would tell her what to do about the children.

Chapter Nine

"Hi, Dad. You're up a little late, aren't you?

"Kirsten, it's not your dad, it's Margaret McFarland. I'm at the hospital where your dad was taken after he had an accident. He's—"

"Accident? What kind of accident? Is he okay?"

"He's alive but unconscious. He fell into the swimming pool trying to rescue a friend of the children."

"Unconscious? Is he going to be okay?"

Margaret could hear a male voice in the background at the other end of the line, then Kirsten repeating what she had just been told.

"Where are Kelly and Sean? Are they okay?"

"They're right here and I'll let you talk to them in a minute. Clarke has stable vital signs but he hasn't come to since I pulled him from the water. They are doing various tests on him for brain trauma, but it's been a while now. I'm hoping they'll come out soon with more information."

"Brain trauma? Did he hit his head?"

"No, I don't think so, but he was under the water long enough to deprive his brain of oxygen for several seconds. I tried to resuscitate him before the paramedics arrived, but he didn't respond."

"Can I talk to the children?"

"Of course."

Margaret handed the phone to Sean and he immediately put

it on speaker phone so his sister could hear and talk also.

"Mom? Mom I'm so scared. I don't want Grandpa to die." Sean was sobbing as he got the words out.

"Darling, your dad and I will get there as quickly as we can. You know Grandpa is in the best place where he'll get the best care until we can catch a plane."

"How soon can you come home? What if Grandpa wakes up and you're not here?"

"Don't worry, Mom." Kelly spoke into the phone her brother was holding. "If Grandpa wakes up, Peggy will be here. He'll be happy to see her because he loves her. She's taking good care of us, too, Mom. She brushes my hair when I wash it and she lets me wear her nail polish. She lets Sean sit down before her at the table so he doesn't have to the do the dishes. You know what Grandpa's rules are."

Margaret held her breath. Kelly was going on and on about how close Clarke and the children were to her. She was tempted to take the phone and apologize to Kirsten but it was obvious the child was trying to reassure her mother that they would all be fine until her parents could get home. It was all nervous chatter.

Kirsten finally cut in to Kelly's oratory. "Sweetie pie, I will talk to Margaret about your supervision. She may not be up to caring for you on her own. I'm happy you are enjoying her company, but it may be a few days before we can get out of here and that's a long time to ask a stranger to babysit. Besides, she might want to sit with Grandpa by herself.

"You and your brother could go to the Burnstroms' until we get home. They've always welcomed you when Grandpa couldn't stay with you. Your daddy and I will get there just as fast as we can. Love you, sweethearts. Now put Mrs. McFarland back on the phone so we can discuss this."

"Love you too, Mommy." Said in unison, then Sean added, "Please let Maggie stay with us. We want her there. We don't want to go to the Burnstroms'."

On that note, he took the phone off speaker and handed it back to Margaret.

"I'm sorry, Kirsten. I don't want to upset any plans you feel are best for the children."

"There is no need to apologize, Margaret. I feel better knowing the children are comfortable with you. However, if you are planning on staying in Hamilton to be with Dad, Kelly and Sean have to know they can't take up all the time you would rather spend at the hospital."

"If you prefer they go to the neighbour's, then I will take a hotel room near the hospital. I wondered if there were any family members that might come and stay with them. They might be more comfortable with an aunt or uncle?"

"Mitch's only sibling, his sister Claire, lives in Yorkshire, England. The kids have only met her three or four times. They've stayed with our neighbours a number of times, so I think that's probably the best place for them. I'll call and make the arrangements. You are welcome to stay at the house if you like. I don't want you going to the expense of a hotel."

"I'll be happy to stay with the children tonight, once we know that Clarke is out of the woods. Do you mind if they stay at the hospital with me until they can see him, whether he's awake or not? I'll tuck them in on a sofa with a pillow and quilt. I don't think they're ready to go home just yet. Nor am I."

"Of course. Exactly what happened?"

Margaret went on to explain the happenings of the evening and how Clarke had been trapped under his wheelchair. She felt negligent when telling of chatting on the phone and Kelly having to come and fetch her. It really wasn't her fault, but she couldn't help thinking it would have had a different outcome if Clarke had not been left to watch a number of children alone.

After assuring Kirsten that the other child was a little scared by her own near drowning but none the worse for wear, they agreed that Margaret and the two children would remain at the hospital until word was received on Clarke's situation. While they had been talking, Mitchell had already started the wheels in motion for their long trip home.

Chapter Ten

It was two o'clock in the morning when a doctor squeezed Margaret's shoulder to awaken her. It took a few seconds to recognize her surroundings and remember where she was and why. The doctor motioned to her to follow him into the hallway.

"I'm Doctor Kettridge, Roger Kettridge."

He looked about mid-thirties, stalky and dimples in both cheeks. His voice was soft and his touch gentle.

"You're Mr. Ingram's next of kin?"

"No. I'm a close friend. I'm actually a guest in his daughter's home right now."

"Is his daughter here, in the hospital?"

"No. She is out of the country. Mr. Ingram had invited me to stay with him to help with his grandchildren while their parents worked at a mission in Peru."

"They're the children asleep in the lounge?"

"Yes. They wanted to stay until they knew their grandfather was going to be okay."

"His vitals are stable and there is no outward sign of trauma. We're giving him oxygen. His lungs could become infected from the water he inhaled and we want to make sure his brain is receiving a sufficient amount of oxygen. His coma is caused by hypoxia or lack of oxygen to the brain. We're monitoring him and the next twenty-four hours will give us a better indication of his prognosis. Is his family planning on returning to Hamilton?"

"Yes. I spoke with them and they are in the process of

making travel arrangements. They are in a remote area and have to travel a distance to reach an airport, so it may be a few days before they arrive."

She looked toward the flush-cheeked children sleeping on the two sofas. "Can the children and I see him? I would like to take them home, but they want to see that he's breathing and alive before they leave."

"Of course. Will it bother them to see him hooked up to various pieces of equipment?"

"It may, but I don't think they'll leave until they can see him with their own eyes."

"I'll tell the nurse to let them in for five minutes."

"Will we be able to sit with him tomorrow if he's still not awake?"

"As long as the children can do so without disturbing him. And just for short periods of time."

Margaret gently shook the children and told them what the doctor had said. They were excited about getting to see him. After cautioning them about the noises made by the hospital equipment and the tubes attached to their grandfather, she took them to the nursing station.

Sean's eyes rounded to saucers when they approached the glass-windowed room. Kelly tightened her grip on Margaret's hand. They moved to one side of the bed in silence. Finally, Kelly moved closer to her grandfather's head and whispered, "Grandpa, I am so sorry we let you fall into the pool. I'm sorry we couldn't get you out faster. Peggie saved you." She started to sob softly.

Sean didn't move any closer. He never stopped staring at the old man. Finally, he said with conviction. "You're not going to die, Grandpa. I won't let you. Mom will be mad at you if she comes home and you're not here. You can't die. You just can't." He turned and fled into the hallway away from the windowed room.

Kelly went out to hug Sean while Margaret touched Clarke's hand. "You sleep well, my darling. You'll need your strength for when you wake up. Those children are not going to leave you alone for a minute."

She kissed his cheek and whispered, "I'll be back to tomorrow and hopefully you will be wide eyed and giving the nurses a hard time about wanting to go home."

Chapter Eleven

"Margaret, that's horrible! Oh dear, what can I do?" Helen's concern was genuine. Margaret knew she would have jumped on the next plane to Hamilton if asked. All of them would have.

Her friends had gathered in Helen's condo at her request. It was easier to explain the events of the previous evening to all of them at once.

"What are you going to do?"

"Will you stay there until Clarke's daughter arrives?"

"Where will you stay?"

The questions were coming fast and furious.

"There is nothing any of you can do for now except to water my plants and collect my mail, please. I will stay as long as Clarke needs me. His daughter has offered me the guest room in her home, indefinitely. The children want me to stay here as well. A neighbour has offered to take them, but they want to stay with me."

"Margaret, won't it be difficult for you to care for two children under the circumstances? I think you should insist they go to the neighbour's."

"Olivia, I appreciate your concern for me but the children are old enough not to be a bother. They are so upset about their grandfather, they were arguing over who would sleep in his room and look after it until he's released from the hospital. They are also worried I will leave and not come back."

"But …"

"No buts. I'm staying right here … and so are the children. Actually, I need them as much as they need me. They are frightened. Think about it! Their grandfather is lying in a coma in hospital. Their parents are thousands of miles away and having difficulty getting out of the location where they're working. The neighbours have no real connection to Clarke. The children accept the fact that Clarke and I love each other and that automatically puts me front and centre in their eyes as the closest thing to family they have at this point. They … I … well, they're the closest thing I have to grandchildren and I've become quite fond of them. They are comforting to me in their own way and give me the focus I need to keep me from falling apart right now."

"But what about when you are at the hospital? Can they go to the neighbour's at least during the day?" Sarah was always the practical one.

"We haven't worked out the logistics yet but they may be able to come for part of the day at least."

Helen joined the conversation again with an affirmation of understanding. "Margaret, you seem to have the situation well in hand. Those kids need a constant in their lives right now and it looks like you're it. I'll pray that Clarke regains consciousness quickly and I think his family is so lucky to have you in their lives. You keep hugging those kids and giving them the love they're used to receiving from their grandpa. Just remember, if you need us, we are only an hour away by airplane. Keep strong my friend."

The others gave their dittos to Helen's offer and as the telephone connection was closed Margaret considered once again how much she was blessed to have such caring friends.

Now, back to the problems at hand. Margaret dialled the number for the hospital.

Chapter Twelve

Clarke had not regained consciousness. There were no changes to his condition. She had just replaced the phone on its base when it rang.

"Margaret, this is Kirsten. Have you any news on my dad?"

"Good morning, Kirsten. I just hung up the phone after calling the hospital and, unfortunately, there is no change in his condition. They tell me not to be too concerned as it's still early after his accident. All they can do is continue to monitor him."

"Did they say what will happen if he doesn't wake up soon?"

"They don't go into too much detail with me, Kirsten. I'm not his next of kin and I think the only reason they are talking to me at all is because of the children and the fact that I'm in touch with you. Maybe if you called the hospital you might get more out of them."

"I think that's what I'll do. We have to get to Lima to catch a plane and there isn't too much to choose from in the way of transportation from here. We're in a rather remote position but there is a small airport, however the weather isn't great today. Some of the shared taxis are reluctant to take us in that direction because of some unrest in the mountains. They say it's getting dangerous. If we take a mini-bus it might take us several days to get there because of a layover. In any event, I won't have cell phone connection. The only reason we have it here is through the Wi-Fi at the hotel in the village. I'll call the hospital and get back to you."

Margaret got the children up, gave them breakfast while they waited for Kirsten to call back. It was almost noon before the phone rang.

Kirsten explained that the doctors had no way of knowing how long it might take Clarke to wake up. It could be hours, days or weeks.

"In the meantime, Margaret, I am going to the hotel now to fax a power-of-attorney to the hospital authorizing them to allow you full responsibility for Dad's care until we can get there. I phoned our lawyer and he will send a copy of my power-of-attorney to their office also so that they will have the full chain of authority. I know how difficult it can be sometimes making the right connections to get out from here. Sometimes it depends on the weather, the road conditions due to minor earthquakes, or political goings on."

"You are placing an awful lot of responsibility on me, Kirsten. We've never met. Are you sure you want to give me this much power over your dad's care? I will do everything I can to make sure he's well taken care of, but still, I hope you have thought this through."

"Margaret, I have no choice. My dad has spoken so highly of you and hinted that he hoped you and he might have a future together. He has always had excellent instincts, so I have to trust him and his gut feelings. If anything were to change while Mitch and I are travelling and unreachable, I want to know someone who cares is there and can make decisions on his and my behalf. While I think of it, I'd better include the children's health care on that power-of-attorney. I'm sorry to dump this on you, but Dad only has me and these are the things you just don't think about until it happens. If you would rather not, I will understand and ask one of our friends to do it."

"I'll do anything I can for you, Clarke, and the children. You will be home in a few days and hopefully he will wake up and be able to make his own decisions before then."

"Thank you. I'm eager to get on the road. Things change down here in a matter of minutes and I want to be ready to go as soon as a mode of transportation becomes available. If you don't hear from me again, you'll know we found a ride and are on our way. Let me talk to the children for a few minutes please before I hang up."

The children were ecstatic to learn their parents would be on their way home soon. The phone rang again before they could leave for the hospital. It was Kirsten's lawyer asking her to drop into his office to sign and pick up some papers.

It was mid-afternoon when they finally arrived at the hospital. They had to buzz and wait to be allowed into the section and then sit in the visitors' lounge until they were allowed in to Clarke's room. Normally, only one person at a time was allowed to visit but exception was made for Margaret and the children as long as they remained quiet. They could visit for fifteen minutes at the top of every hour.

He looked pale, but the children spoke in terms of him sleeping. They each took turns carrying on softly spoken conversations. Sean was especially eager that Clarke know about the Blue Jays four game home series starting that evening and that he'd be sure to watch it and relay the score and all the major plays. Their time was up before they were prepared for it, but they didn't whine, fearful of not being allowed back in.

"What will we do while we wait for the next hour, Peggy?"

"I brought some bottles of water and we can drink them outside in the little park on the grounds. I also brought playing cards. Let's see if there's a table available."

"What if Grandpa wakes up while we're out here?" Sean was reluctantly following them through the doors to the sidewalk.

"Then we'll have a wonderful surprise when we go back

inside."

When they found the green space and settled on one of a number of tables available, Margaret thought it was time for them to be told about the possibility of a long vigil at the bedside of their grandfather.

"... but he *could* wake up any minute, right?"

Margaret's heart went out to this little man who wanted so desperately for his grandfather to wake up *now* rather than days or weeks from now.

"Right, he could. However, we must be prepared in case he doesn't. I don't want you to be too disappointed each time you go into his room."

"What happens if he doesn't?" Kelly was playing with a leaf that had floated onto the table from one of the nearby trees.

They were sitting in a large green area surrounded by buildings. There were several trees and paths. It was an oasis, a quiet place for staff or visitors to sit and relax — enjoy some down time from the strain that involved everyone who had a reason to be inside the brick walls.

"Then we have to keeping visiting and praying. Maybe tomorrow we can bring some magazines or a newspaper with all the sporting events your grandfather is interested in. You can read them to him so that he won't miss anything."

"Yes. Maybe he'll hear us and wake up. If he's sleeping, he can't help it. He'll have to wake up." The hope that was resonating in Sean's young voice was enough to make Margaret want to hug him so close to heart. Instead she had to bring him back to reality.

"He's not sleeping in the way we think of sleeping. He's in a deeper sleep that he can't just shake himself awake from. His brain is resting. It's tired from being without oxygen and it needs time to heal itself. When it's ready, it will let your grandfather know it's time to open his eyes and face the world again."

"But you told us he might be able to hear us. If he can, why doesn't he let us know so we won't be worried and we can let him just sleep." The hope in his voice had turned to impatience.

"He has no control over what he can and can't do right now. We just have to be patient."

Margaret opened the bag she had set on the table. "Now who wants to try to beat me at gin rummy?"

Chapter Thirteen

Three more days went by with no change in Clarke and no word from Kirsten and Mitchell. Margaret tried phoning them a couple of times only to hear the call ring through. The children had been perfect companions at the hospital and filled the hours at home. Kelly had taken to looking up things on the computer. Margaret hoped the answers she found helped her to understand rather than confuse or frighten her. Sean cut out articles that he thought would interest his grandfather and religiously read them to him.

Margaret's friends took turns calling daily.

"Don't the children have to return to school in a few weeks?" Olivia voiced a concern that had surfaced the day before.

"Yes. Kelly remarked that some of her friends already had been shopping with their mothers for new school clothes. She said her mother always bought them on sale in the middle of August which means now. I don't know if that's a hint that I should be taking her shopping or if she's just letting me know that her mother should be home soon."

"Was her mother planning on being home by now?"

"I believe they still had another week in their commitment to the mission but that would still give her plenty of time to outfit the kids before school. I'm hoping they'll be somewhere with phone service by tomorrow."

"People sure have to be dedicated to go into those areas of the world. It's hard to believe in this day and age that remoteness like that still exists. I give them a lot of credit. Oh well, they know where they aren't even if you don't. I give you credit, too, kiddo, for taking care of those children."

"They really are no problem. I remember Clarke telling me that they practically look after themselves and they do. I'm going to have a hard time saying goodbye when the time comes."

"You're not thinking of moving down there are you?" Olivia sounded concerned more than curious.

"No, of course not. You're forgetting that Clarke's home is in Ottawa. I'm sure once he's awake and feeling stronger, he'll want to go home and have his own doctors there care for him."

"I suppose. Margaret, just don't forget to take care of yourself. All this stress can take its toll and I wouldn't want to hear next that you're in the hospital."

"Don't worry about me, Olivia. It does me good to look after others for a change. I spent too many years thinking only about me. Besides, these children take very good care of me. If they could stay to tuck me in at night, they would. Say hi to the other girls for me. I'll be in touch as soon as I know anything more."

Chapter Fourteen

That afternoon when the three went to the hospital they were surprised to see Clarke lying in bed with only an IV attached.

"Grandpa! Grandpa!" The children ran to his side and grabbed his hand.

Margaret backed up onto the foot of a nurse who was following them in.

"Mrs. McFarland, I just tried calling you."

"Peggy, is Grandpa just sleeping now?"

Margaret called the two worried looking youngsters into the hallway. "Why don't you wait in the visitors' room until I talk with the nurse?"

"But …"

"Come on, Kelly. Maggie will tell us what's going on after." Sean tugged Kelly's sleeve and the two of them walked down the hall and into the other room.

"What's happening with Clarke?"

"The doctor is in the hospital and will be here shortly to talk to you. All I can tell you is that Mr. Ingram is still in a coma but the need for assisted breathing is no longer there. That sometimes happens with patients who have suffered his type of trauma, but I don't want to guess at things. Best we wait for Doctor Kettridge and you can ask him your questions."

Margaret went back into Clarke's room. She walked to the side of the bed and took his hand.

"Clarke, I'm so happy to see you breathing on your own."

No response. That hadn't changed.

Margaret almost burst into tears.

"Mrs. McFarland." The doctor approached her. "I'm happy you're here. We have some things to discuss about Mr. Ingram's care."

❦ ❦ ❦

Margaret learned that because Clarke was breathing strongly and steadily on his own, he was taken off the respirator. His inability to take food necessitated the IV tube through which he received his nutrition and some medications. This was not necessarily a totally good thing, however.

"He will be moved out of the intensive care unit to a regular room on another floor and his brain activity will continue to be monitored."

"Does this mean he's showing signs of improving? Of possibly waking from the coma soon?" Margaret was hoping to hear a positive answer.

"Not, really. He's stable and showing no signs of deteriorating but neither is he improving." Dr. Kettridge looked at Clarke's chart.

"As I said, we'll move him and continue the same type of surveillance in the hope that something will change soon."

"And if it doesn't?"

"Then he will possibly be moved to another facility that can continue his care for the long term."

Margaret gasped. "Long term?"

"Mrs. McFarland, we are an urgent care hospital. He would be better served at a long-term care facility. With this type of trauma, Mr. Ingram could still wake up at any time, but I must be honest. If there is no response after three or four days, seven at the outside, it's been our experience that the patient may remain comatose for months. Maybe even years. I'm sorry but you must be aware of what could lay ahead."

Margaret felt faint. This couldn't be happening. Not to Clarke. He was so full of life. He loved and lived every day to its limit. Surely he hadn't survived everything he had suffered with a smile only to spend the rest of his days in bed asleep.

The children! Dear God what will I tell the children?

"Have you any word on when Mr. Ingram's family will arrive?"

"What?" She realized the doctor was waiting for answer to a question.

"Mr. Ingram's family. Are they expected to arrive soon?"

"His family? No. No, it's strange. I thought I would have heard from them by now. If I don't hear anything today, I will try to contact their church or the agency that the church works with to see if they've even been able to leave the village yet.

"I ... I don't know what to tell the children. Shall I tell them he's still sleeping but not as deeply now?"

"If they are sensitive children you may want to keep it that simple. If they are able to cope with more, then you may want to tell them exactly what I've told you. They are old enough to catch on. Children are far more intelligent than we give them credit for sometimes. They may be angry if you don't level with them."

"Oh dear. I was hoping their parents would be here by now to deal with this. I'm not experienced with children. I don't know if I can find the right words."

"The words will come. They seem like sensible young people to me." He took her by the elbow and started walking her toward the waiting room. "Mr. Ingram will be here for a couple more days. Maybe he'll wake up in the meantime."

The doctor patted her hand and left her in the doorway facing two sets of questioning eyes.

"Is Grandpa getting better, Peggy?" Kelly was working the front of her T-shirt into a knot.

Margaret smiled and sat in a chair opposite them.

"You know that God doesn't always answer our prayers in the way we want him to. Sometimes he takes a roundabout route that takes a little longer to get to where we want to be."

Two heads nodded in slow unison.

"Well, that's what's happening here. The good news is that your grandfather's lungs are strong enough to work on their own. He doesn't need the respirator anymore. The sad news is that his brain isn't quite ready to let him wake up yet. That may take a little longer than we first thought or hoped."

"How much longer?"

"The doctor doesn't know. He said it could still happen any minute and then again it might take a while longer."

Sean stood up. "You mean Grandpa may never wake up!"

The room was small with two leather sofas and three chairs lining the walls. Sean paced the perimeter twice before he stopped directly in front of Margaret. "You're lying to us. You keep saying he can wake up any minute but you know very well he's never going to wake up. You're a liar. I hate you!" Tears followed then he broke into a run toward the old man's room.

Kelly called after him. "Sean, wait. You don't mean that."

Margaret watched the two poor, broken-hearted children run to the man they loved so much. Her heart was aching — for the children and for herself. Was she going to lose this kind, gentle man who made her laugh and helped her see how beautiful life could be if you let it? She had only known him a few months. His grandchildren had known him all their lives.

She only hoped their parents were on a plane heading north to help soothe their poor over-worked minds. It was a hard thing for her, an adult, to deal with. She was so angry herself how could she expect two small children not to show anger at life's cruel blow.

The nurse bent the rules a little and allowed the children to sit quietly staring at their grandfather beyond the allotted time. Margaret knew the staff understood what must be going through their minds.

After a half hour, Sean came sheepishly to stand in front of her. "I'm sorry, Peggy. I know it's not your fault. You're only telling us what the doctor said. I don't hate you."

"I know you didn't mean it, Sean. You love your grandpa so much it's hard to watch him sleep on and on. I'm sure you would rather he wake up and tell you silly jokes and stories. I want him to wake up, too."

Kelly looked out the window. "What's taking Mom and Dad so long to get here? They should have been somewhere that we can talk to them by now."

"Maybe that's what Grandpa's brain is waiting for. It's saving his strength until they get home."

"If we don't hear from your parents by late this afternoon, I'll call your pastor and find out if there's someone we can contact at the agency that sponsors these missions."

"Yes. Last year there was a road washout that kept them there a day longer. Remember Sean?"

❤❤❤

When she spoke to the pastor after they arrived home in the late afternoon, he promised to do whatever he could to try to pinpoint where they might be on their journey out of Satipo Province in Peru.

Later that night, after the children had gone to bed, Margaret turned on the late news as a news story was breaking from Peru that a mini-bus had disappeared in the mountains in Satipo Province, Peru.

Chapter Fifteen

"I am coming down on the next plane. No arguments from you this time either. I'm packing as we speak." Margaret could hear the anxiety and determination in Olivia's voice.

"I won't argue with you, Olivia. I can use a hug from a friend right about now."

"Those poor children. And poor, poor you. I will stay with you, on the sofa if need be, so you don't have to shoulder this alone. Give me the address again. I don't want you having to drive to the airport."

"It's a small airport. It's no big deal and it will give the kids something to see besides the hospital and this house."

"Has no one from the neighbourhood or their church offered to help with the children?"

"Yes, of course they have. The children are so frightened right now they don't want to be with anyone but me. I do believe they're afraid to let me out of their sight in case I disappear too. Some women from the church have brought baking and casseroles and offered to sit with the children so I can go to the hospital unencumbered. Two of the neighbours insisted the children stay at their homes until Kirsten and Mitchell are found and arrive back home. I couldn't nor wouldn't let them go. We need each other right now. I don't know what I would do with myself if they weren't around. Everyone is trying to help each in their own way."

"I'm going to hang up now so I can book a flight and get to

the airport. If I can't get a direct flight to Hamilton, then I'll take one to Toronto and either get a connecting flight or take the train. I'll be in touch once I'm on my way. Margaret, honey, take good care of yourself. Help is on the way."

Margaret placed the phone on the stand and took several deep breaths. Her friends had been flabbergasted when she called them this morning with this turn of events. They were concerned that she was caught in the middle of it all and it might prove too much for her. First Clarke, then the responsibility of the children, and now the missing parents. Clarke. One instant she wished he were here to help deal with the situation then in the next instant she was almost happy he wasn't. *You sleep, my darling. By the time you wake up everything will be back to normal — your daughter and her husband will be home, the children will be in their arms and I ... well, I'll be by your bedside waiting for you to open your eyes and smile at me. "Well done, Maggie," you'll say and squeeze my hand.*

The doorbell shook her from her reverie. A man in a dark suit and stark white shirt stood outside the door. His sombre look told her he wasn't about to produce a pie or another macaroni casserole.

"Mrs. McFarland?" He extended a hand.

"Yes." Margaret accepted his firm grip in a business-like handshake.

"I'm Malcolm Wright from the Bible Mission and a member of the Sennetts' congregation. I just came from speaking with Pastor Schmidt. If you have time right now, I'll tell you what I know about the situation in Peru."

The children were playing in their neighbour's yard so Margaret invited the man in and offered him some iced tea. She noticed he walked with a slight limp and one eye drooped a little.

"The bus the Sennetts were in apparently went over an embankment in the mountains in the western part of the province. The reports coming out say there are survivors even though it's been down there unseen for a couple of days. But it's very difficult terrain to access and it may take another day to lift everyone out. We have no way of knowing who the passengers are but considering we haven't heard from Mitchell or Kirsten and the timing is right, we can only assume they were on that bus. There is a small airport near the city of Satipo and I had assumed that was the mode of transportation they would have taken. They were working not far away but I've been told the weather wasn't great and all planes had been grounded. I guess they decided it might be faster to take the bus out. Lima, where the major airport for Peru is, is about ten or eleven hours away by road.

"Our agency is being kept abreast of the situation by the authorities and as soon as we know anything more I'll be in touch with you and Pastor Schmidt. Are you or the children in need of anything? Do you have groceries? Are you able to get to the hospital to see Mr. Ingram?"

"We're fine. A friend of mine is on her way from Ottawa to help me and to stay with the children when need be. Any news that you can give us about Kirsten and Mitchell will be most welcome. Kelly and Sean are so frightened that their parents might not return, they hardly leave my side. It was bad enough with their grandfather so seriously ill but now they are absolutely devastated. I'm surprised they have stayed this long at the neighbour's house.

"I try to keep them away from the television but they're old enough to know when the news is being shown and are disappointed each time nothing new is reported."

"Once our agency knows anything at all about their injuries, if any, and location, I'll call. Our people down there will help with the orchestration of their rescue, hospitalization if necessary, and then their transportation home. In the meantime, we must all place our faith in the Saviour."

"Thank you for coming by rather than phoning. It's more

comforting to see the person one is dealing with rather than listening to a voice on the other end of a line."

"I'll continue to stay in touch, Mrs. McFarland."

A few minutes after she closed the door behind him, the phone rang. "I can't get a decent flight but I can make the next train if all the traffic lights are green between here and the station. I'll get into Hamilton about 7:30 this evening. Gerald is bringing the car around now."

"I'll be there. You have the number for Clarke's cell phone if you need me. The kids and I will go to the hospital this afternoon and stay through until train time."

Margaret breathed a sigh of relief. Olivia hadn't hesitated. As soon as she was needed, she had dropped everything to come to the aid of her friend. *Thank you, God, for giving me such caring friends.*

Chapter Sixteen

It was almost lunch time when the phone rang again. Someone from hospital administration wanted to see her later that day.

She and the kids had been taking the bus to the hospital. Parking was difficult and expensive, and it was not far to public transit at either end, but today they took the car so they could go straight to the train station to pick up Olivia.

The woman who had called wanted to discuss the transfer of Clarke to the long-term rehabilitation facility that housed the acquired brain injury services.

"Long-term care? He's been in here less than a week. I would think he still needs acute care."

"He is being fed intravenously and his vitals need checking regularly. Unfortunately, that doesn't constitute acute care. The alternate care facilities are fully equipped should an emergency arise, and they are attached to the General Hospital by a bridge. Mrs. McFarland, I understand your concern about transferring him, but he will receive excellent care where he's going. Other acute care patients are waiting for beds to open and one who has been awaiting major surgery is scheduled to move into that bed tomorrow."

"Tomorrow? That soon? I thought the doctor said it might take up to seven days."

"Mr. Ingram is stable, and there is space for him at the other facility. We must move him before it's gone to another patient. He'll probably be moved sometime late this evening."

"Where will he be moved and how?"

"He will be moved on a gurney to the other facility. He won't even be taken outside. The doctors on that side are excellent and Mr. Ingram will receive the utmost care."

"Will his grandchildren be allowed to visit?"

"Yes. The visitation for family is less restricted than in here."

"It seems he's being moved to a storage facility where we wait and see what happens."

"It's not like that at all. He will receive the same level of care as he would if he remained here. He's been removed from all the emergency equipment that was necessary to bring him to this level, he no longer needs the constant fifteen-minute monitoring and adjustments."

Margaret reluctantly signed the papers for his transferal. Her only other option was to have him placed in a private care facility where the cost is not covered by the government. She knew that was beyond the realm of Clarke's financial capability. In her heart she felt that if Clarke could make the decision, he probably would rather be in Ottawa under the care of his own doctor and where his numerous friends could visit.

The woman gave her a map of the facility and told her where to park and which entrance to use after today. The children had been waiting in the outer office and now they were full of questions. Margaret assured them, their grandfather was going to be just as comfortable in the new location and that it would be better visiting times with fewer restrictions.

Clarke lay in his continuing state of repose as the children told him all about his upcoming move to another part of the hospital. Margaret watched and marvelled at the flexibility or maybe it was adaptability of children. She had been upset at the thought of his being moved around like a car on a used car lot. The red one needs to be front and centre today but tomorrow it will be replaced by the blue one because that one will need the exposure. The red one will still be advertised and polished but just not given the same level of attention as it is today.

They moved in and out of his room at the required times and before she knew it, it was supper time. Olivia had texted once she was aboard the train to confirm she had indeed made it.

Kelly was just returning to the waiting room when the phone in Margaret's hand began ringing.

"I'll be late arriving. We've been delayed by a protest group who have set up a road block on the railway tracks. Apparently, they're not causing complete stoppage of trains, only delays but no one seems to know how long this one will la—"

"Mrs. McFarland, I'm glad I caught you. Mr. Ingram has opened his eyes." The nurse was waving her to come.

"Grandpa's awake?" Sean darted for the doorway.

"Margaret? Margaret, are you there? What's going on? Did you hear me? I'll be la—"

"There's the doctor now. Come" The nurse started down the hallway.

"Olivia, I'll call you back shortly. It looks like Clarke has gained consciousness."

"Peggy, let's go. Grandpa's awake and we're not there. He'll wonder why." Sean had tears in his eyes but was smiling.

"Oh my …" Olivia was uncharacteristically lost for words.

Margaret broke the connection on a sputtering Olivia. Sean and Kelly had both of her arms firmly in their grips and were pulling her down the hall.

They arrived at Clarke's room only to have the nurse block their entrance. "Just give the doctor a minute or two to examine the patient."

The children had their faces pressed against the glass windows staring into his room. "His eyes are open. His eyes are open."

Margaret burst out in giggles. Her Clarke was awake. *He's awake. Thank you, Lord.*

The doctor looked in both eyes then carried out a few movements with Clarke's arms and feet. They watched as the nurse took his blood pressure and pulse. The doctor appeared to be talking to Clarke then finally turned and waved Margaret and the children in.

"Grandpa! We knew you'd wake up soon." Kelly moved to the side of the bed with her brother standing open-mouthed beside her.

Margaret remained at the foot of the bed apprehensively studying Clarke's face.

"Kelly, Sean, what are you doing here?"

"We were waiting for you to wake up." Sean took a step closer.

"Wake up? Was I sleeping? What am I doing here?"

"You're in the hospital, Grandpa. Don't you remember? You fell into the swimming pool?"

"Swimming pool? I did?"

"Peggy saved you. You almost drowned."

"Who's Peggy?"

Chapter Seventeen

The doctor, who had been writing on the chart, looked up. "Who is Peggy?" he whispered to Margaret.

"Me."

The doctor moved closer to Clarke, gently shuffling the children to the foot of the bed.

"Mr. Ingram, do you recognize the woman standing at the foot of your bed?"

Margaret held her breath while Clarke looked at her.

"Yes. That's my friend. I think. I can't remember her name but her face is familiar."

The children both gasped and looked at Margaret.

The doctor asked the nurse to take the children out of the room while he, the patient and Mrs. McFarland had a little conversation. He then motioned Margaret to speak to Clarke.

She moved to the side of the bed and took one of Clarke's hands in her own.

"Clarke, darling, I'm so happy you finally decided to wake up and join us once again."

Clarke appeared startled for a moment. "You seem so familiar but I'm afraid I'm not sure who you are. The children mentioned someone named Peggy, are you she?"

Margaret smiled. "I'm Margaret McFarland. You usually call me Maggie. The children call me Peggy."

"Maggie. Maggie." He repeated the name a couple more times. "Why do the children call you Peggy?"

Her heart was hurting from the small crack working its way through it.

The doctor spoke up. "You do know who those children are don't you?"

"My grandchildren."

"You know them and you know who you are and your birthday. What else do you remember?"

Clarke closed his eyes as if working at remembering.

"I don't know. Can you give me a hint?"

"Do you know what city you're in?"

"Since my grandchildren are here, I'm either in Hamilton or Ottawa."

"That's good, Mr. Ingram. That's very good."

"So where am I?"

"You're in Hamilton. You had an accident and fell into the swimming pool at your daughter's house."

"My daughter … Kirsten. Is she here?"

Margaret answered before the doctor did. "Kirsten and Mitchell are in South America working at a mission. That's why we are babysitting your grandchildren."

"We're babysitting? You and I? That's strange."

"Why is it strange?"

"Because …" He studied her face. "I'm sure I know you."

This time the doctor interrupted. "I think we'll forgo any more questions for now. I want you to rest a little, Mr. Ingram. You've been through a major trauma and I don't want you stressed. I think you've done enough talking and thinking for now."

He motioned Margaret toward the door.

"Can the children come in and say good night to their grandfather? They are anxious to know he's okay."

"Just a good night. I'll hold Mr. Ingram here for one more night before we move him. Better he not have another upheaval after just waking up."

While the children were in saying good night the doctor explained that Clarke could very well recognize her the next time he woke up. Or not. His amnesia was not deep and the chances of his remembering everything soon were quite good. They would see what another night brought before making any decision about his ongoing care.

Sean and Kelly were beaming when they left the old man's room.

"You were right, Peggy. Grandpa did wake up and remember us. He said that maybe he'll go home with us tomorrow." Sean seemed quite sure of himself.

"I think the doctor might have something to say about that. Your grandpa just woke up. He's still pretty weak and a wee bit forgetful. You wouldn't want him to come home before he's healthy enough to do so.

"I don't know about you guys but I am starving. What do you say we go for supper?"

Chapter Eighteen

"Does your friend have grey hair too?" Kelly was craning her neck looking at the passengers departing the train. "No. She has blonde hair."

"Oh, so she's quite a bit younger than you."

Margaret was about to make a remark but decided there was no need for sarcasm. The children would never understand the money and effort Olivia put into her passion for continuing to look young and attractive.

"Is that her?" Sean pointed to a beautiful twenty-something young woman coming through the glass door from the platform.

"No. She's a little older than that." Margaret smiled.

"Margaret!" The voice was followed by a harried looking Olivia.

"Olivia, welcome." Hugs were exchanged then the children introduced.

"Peggy said that your train was held up. Were they robbers, Mrs. Kovacs?"

"I'm not married, Sean, so you can call me Olivia, and no, they weren't robbers."

"Who were they?"

Margaret interjected. "They were some people who were trying to get attention so they held a peaceful demonstration."

"A demonstration on a railway track?" Kelly looked puzzled. "When our teacher gives us a demonstration on something, it's usually on the blackboard."

"It was a different kind of demonstration, Kelly. We can talk more about it tomorrow. I'll bet Olivia would really like to get home and have a nice bath and maybe something to eat."

"Our grandpa has been in a coma for almost a week but he woke up tonight." Sean reached for one of Olivia's bags.

"I like your purse, Olivia. Jungle print is my favourite." Kelly reached for another of the bags and began rolling it toward the door.

❦ ❦ ❦

"Honestly, Margaret, I don't know why you didn't let me come sooner. I don't know how you've handled all this by yourself. Those kids are adorable, but they do require a lot of attention and then all this with Clarke and now the kids' parents. I don't think you signed on for all of this."

"I guess I've been going on adrenaline, Olivia. Sean and Kelly have been really good. I don't know that I would have reacted as well when I was a child. I think it helps that they have each other and are so close in age."

"They adore you. I can see that. Kelly told me she wishes you could be her for-real grandmother."

Olivia had bathed and changed into a nightshirt and slippers. Margaret and the kids had heated leftovers from a casserole a neighbour had brought over the day before. The children were in the family room watching one of their taped shows.

"What's the latest on their parents?"

"The man from the agency called while you were in the bathtub. Apparently, they've lost communication with the rescue team. They're trying to find out where the injured are being taken so they can sort out how many survived and who they are. It's difficult at the best of times because not all the areas down there have land lines and almost zilch as far as Internet reception.

"I only hope we have good news before we see Clarke again.

I don't know how he will respond to a catastrophe involving his only child and her husband."

Margaret laced her fingers together and fidgeted with her rings. Before her friend could respond she looked at Olivia and sighed. "I am so, so happy you are here. Now that everything is coming to a head, I will welcome your support more than you can know."

"We'll get through it. You've already handled everything thrown at you with such strength, you must be exhausted. Let me help you over the next hurdles." Olivia moved to the sofa where her friend was struggling to maintain her composure and placed an arm around her shoulders. "Now, why don't you go to bed and get some much-needed rest while I make the kids a bedtime snack."

❦ ❦ ❦

After an hour or so of playing old-fashioned monopoly with the two youngsters, Olivia found some lemons in the refrigerator and made lemonade for them. Second guessing whether lemons had high natural sugar content, she hesitated only a second before pouring them each a tall glass with lots of ice. *Screw the sugar. These kids have a lot worse things on their plates.*

The house phone rang as Olivia was saying good night to Kelly. It rang three times before she heard Margaret's voice from another room. Kelly grabbed her arm before she could leave the room. The girl had stark terror written on her face. "I'm so afraid my mom and dad are dead."

Chapter Nineteen

"It's worse than I ever thought." Margaret was standing by the patio doors staring at the moon's reflection on the pool.

Sean had already been asleep when the call came through. Kelly was lying quietly in bed after being told her mother was safely in the hospital and that there was no word on her dad yet. "I will pray that he's okay too," had been her only words.

"That's all they said? Kirsten is in hospital and Mitchell is still missing?"

Margaret looked toward the stairway leading to the children's bedrooms before replying softly. "Kirsten is in hospital with severe undetermined injuries and Mitchell is MIA along with one other man. They've searched extensively but there is no trace of either of them. They've disappeared into thin air."

"How can that be? If he was thrown from the bus in the accident he can't have rolled that far away that they can't find him or the other guy. If he wandered away, wouldn't they be able to see that also?" Olivia's tone bespoke incredulity.

"I guess the jungle is pretty thick there and maybe it's hard to trace any signs of footsteps. Who knows? In the meantime, Kirsten is in the hospital with only the mission agency to ascertain her care. Pastor Schmidt said there is another Canadian couple in their group, but Kirsten and Mitchell left before the mission was completed. The other couple are still in camp. The Canadian embassy in Lima has been notified and the mission agency has sent someone from the Canadian office down there, but no one really has any authority over her personal care. I guess in this instance since her husband is missing, Clarke would be the next of kin to make any decisions about her medical care. I dread even telling him what has happened. Will he be strong enough or even aware enough to make any decisions? After all, he didn't even recognize me yesterday other than that I vaguely looked familiar to him but he couldn't put a name to my face".

She couldn't hold it in any longer. The tears came, followed by words of desperation. "What am I going to do, Olivia? How can I tell this man who is barely out of a coma that his daughter is critically injured in a South American hospital and that her husband is nowhere to be found? What can he do? Getting around is difficult for him when he's healthy let alone the weakened state he's currently in. What about the children. They have to go back to school in a few weeks. Who is going to look after them? What if their mother is in hospital for weeks or months? What if their father is never found?"

"Whoa. Slow down, Margaret." Olivia guided her to the kitchen where she poured water into the kettle for tea. "First of all, Clarke is in hospital getting the best of care. He must be intelligent enough to know he can't do anything for anybody until he's back on his feet … foot … mobile again. You know what I mean." She looked aghast at how she had handled that solution.

"He's being looked after. As far as we know Kirsten is being cared for in hospital down there. There is nothing can be done for the son-in-law until we know where he is and how he is. So that leaves only the children. I have nothing that needs urgent attention. I can stay with you until the children are in school if need be. Stella and Helen will look after both our condos, collect our mail and cancel the cards and cleaning woman for a few weeks. So that means all we can do is whatever we have control over and that's the children — to a certain degree.

"Talking about the son-in-law, where is his family? Can't they shoulder some of the responsibility of the children?"

"He only has a sister who lives somewhere in England and who, apparently, is planted over there and cannot or will not come back to Canada — for any reason. Kirsten told me they have taken the children over there for two visits but apparently the welcomes were not overly enthusiastic. I got the impression the children were not fond of their British relatives either."

Olivia poured the tea and found some Celebration cookies in the cupboard. She took Margaret's hand and looked her square in the eye. "Well, my dear friend, we have one more urgent issue to deal with right here in this house."

"The children."

"No. That was the last tea bag I used and you know how I get when there is no tea."

Shocked, Margaret stared at her friend for a brief moment before bursting into gales of laughter. She teared up and started fresh every time she looked at the other woman.

"Oh, Olivia. You are exactly what I needed."

She checked on both children before climbing into bed again. With luck, she'd get a few hours of sleep before the phone brought more news — good, bad or otherwise. Margaret was in her bed in the guestroom and Olivia had taken the pull-out bed in the den.

❦ ❦ ❦

"Peggy? Peggy?"

Someone was calling her name.

"Are you awake? Can I come in?"

It was Sean.

"Of course, sweetheart. I'm awake and you can come in and give me a hug."

His cheeks were streaked from dried tears. Margaret's heart just about broke in two looking at the little boy who always tried unsuccessfully to be a strong man. She patted the bed for him to sit down.

"I seem to have a habit of sleeping in. I hope you weren't waiting too long for me to wake up." She gave him a kiss on the cheek and brushed his hair from his forehead. He had a sprinkling of freckles across his nose that she hadn't noticed before. Of course, they were not out of place with his green eyes and golden-coloured hair.

"Is my mother very badly hurt? Will she be able to come home soon?"

"I don't have all the answers yet, Sean. We must first and foremost be grateful to God that she wasn't killed in the crash. At least those prayers were answered. She is in a hospital, so we know she's being well cared for just like your grandpa. I hope we'll find out in the next couple of days just how long it will be before she's strong enough to come home."

The boy appeared to be only a little soothed by her answer. "And my dad? Where is he?"

Oh, dear. What or how much should she tell him? She knew it would only be a matter of time before this became a news item for them to see full screen on the television. Or maybe it wouldn't. Maybe there was enough news out there to keep the reporters from broadcasting that a small bus with two unknown mission volunteers had been involved in an accident.

"They haven't identified which of the injured persons is your dad yet. The good news is, he hasn't been identified among the dead either. He will turn up and be just as eager to see you as you are to see him."

Sean sat with his head down. "Poor Grandpa. Does he know that Mom was in a crash yet?"

"No, but I will tell him today. As a matter of fact, I was going to phone the hospital to see if he's been moved or left in the same room. I may go by myself to have a talk with him. He seemed a bit confused last night, so I thought it might be better if we had a conversation, just the two of us. It might be less stressful for him if I'm the only one in the room he has to remember."

She slipped her robe over her pyjamas and walked with Sean to the stairs. "You go on up and I'll be right there to make you breakfast."

It was then she noticed it was just seven o'clock. No wonder she still felt sleepy. By the time they had all settled down last night she was sure everyone would sleep in. *Oh well, Margaret. Another day of sunshine and surprises.*

Chapter Twenty

She had to wait for about a half hour before she would be allowed in to see Clarke. It was almost a gift. A half hour to herself. Completely to herself. She decided to spend it in the chapel.

The peace and quiet in the little room was exactly what she needed. It felt as if she were in another world. She closed her eyes and searched behind her lids for the water, the pond, the ripple. It wouldn't come. All she saw was Sean's face and eyes. *Shame on you, Margaret. Stop feeling sorry for yourself and think about what those poor, poor children are going through. What's the worst that will happen to you? You might be delayed in Hamilton for a few more weeks then it becomes everyone else's problem, not yours. You will get on a plane and go home with or without Clarke. Your life will go back to where it was before.*

Clarke may never be the same. Even if he recovers fully in both mind and body, he could lose a daughter. He could lose a son-in-law. He may become a full-time guardian to his grandchildren. His life may never be the same.

Kelly and Sean could lose one or both of their parents. One or both parents may live but not regain full health. Their grandfather may never be the same. They may end up being in the care of someone other than their parents or grandfather. Their lives may never be the same — no matter what.

What about Kirsten and Mitchell? Where are they? Will they recover? Fully? Will they be well enough to care for their children? And for an aging and physically handicapped parent?

Possibly all will recover fully and their lives will go back to the way they were before. Bruised but healthy. The odds on that happening were not great. What about financial matters? What will health care costs be? Transportation costs? Long term disability? Emotional distress?

Margaret, you are the lucky one. You should get down on your knees and thank God you are not one of them. Quit feeling put upon. Right now, in the immediate future, you have an elderly man who loves you and needs your care and help. Right now, you have two children who have only you. Only you. Only you. And Olivia. God bless Olivia. Olivia, your friend who came to your aid uninvited. You are two grown women who have been given a job to do. Are you up to it?

Margaret looked around the room. Had she been speaking her thoughts out loud? Who cared. No one else was there. She felt renewed. She *was* the lucky one. Her watch showed that her half hour of contemplation was over. It had been what she needed. She looked up at the ceiling.

You bet your sweet patootie I'm up to it! Look out world — here I come!

Chapter Twenty-one

Clarke was in the same ward but not in the same room. This one was smaller with four beds in it, two occupied and two empty. His head was turned away from her as she approached so she couldn't see if he was sleeping. She hesitated briefly, watching him breathe. He looked long and lean in the bed. She felt her heart skip a beat. It was in that moment she realized just how much she loved this man. *Please God, let him recognize me.*

He turned and smiled.

"Hi handsome. Do you remember me?"

"Yes, of course. You're the beautiful lady that was here yesterday."

She took a deep breath. Okay, so this was not going to be easy but at least he remembered she had been there. There was a single stacking-type chair near the bed so she pulled it over and sat facing him.

"How are you today?"

"I feel pretty good until I try to sit up then I get dizzy."

"I'm not surprised. That poor brain of yours has been through quite an ordeal this past week."

"I understand I fell into a swimming pool and you pulled me out. Is that true?"

"Yes. A child fell into the pool and you tried to save her but your wheelchair went into the pool with you and you became entangled in it."

"Is the child okay?"

"Yes. She's fine. You ended up the only victim in that accident and thank God you are now okay also."

Clarke studied her face. She gave him time to take in all her features. He appeared to be searching for something, anything, familiar.

"Tell me what you remember before your accident." She reached for his hand.

"I know my grandchildren were here yesterday. I know I'm in a hospital in Hamilton and that they live in this city. I know their house and the pool where I understand the accident took place. However, I don't remember the accident at all."

He looked behind her. "Are they not with you today?"

"They will come later. I selfishly wanted some time alone with you before they visit again."

"Why?"

His question took her aback. She wasn't sure how to answer it. Should she forge boldly ahead or take her time and let him form fresh thoughts and opinions about her?

"You don't remember me and that bothers me immensely. I hoped some one-on-one might open up those memory cells."

"I know that I know you, but I don't know how."

"I live in Ottawa where you have your home. We met a couple of months ago and became close friends. You came here to babysit your grandchildren and invited me for a visit. A week into my stay you had this accident and now *I'm* babysitting your grandchildren." She smiled. "Or maybe I should say they are babysitting me. They are adorable and a big help to me since I don't know my way around the city very well."

"You are staying at my daughter's house? Alone with the children?"

"Yes. Don't worry, they love me and I love them. Do you know my name?"

"It's Maggie. Margaret." He appeared to be searching for the rest of her name. "Mc something."

Her heart skipped a beat. "My name is Margaret McFarland. You endearingly took to calling me Maggie and the children have changed that to Peggy."

"Peggy." His eyes lit up. "I remember that. We were in a restaurant."

He appeared to zone out. Margaret could see he was trying to work through his thoughts. She gave him time to absorb the conversation so far.

"What's the last thing you remember?"

"The doctor asked me that. I don't really know. It's like trying to remember where I was three months ago at 2:30 in the afternoon. If I needed an alibi for that day and time, I couldn't give you one. I do know that I *don't* remember being in Hamilton with my grandchildren. I know my home is in Ottawa. I know my address, my telephone number, and my birthday. I remember my life, my friends." He hesitated. "I'm sorry. If I invited you to join me here then I must feel great affection for you. I wish I could remember our relationship."

He appeared quite concerned about hurting her feelings.

"Don't stress over it. You showed me great affection and I care deeply for you, however that will come back to you I'm sure and I don't want to put you in a position of trying to feel something that isn't there right now."

He glanced down at their joined hands but before she could draw hers away, he placed his free hand on top of hers and patted it.

"I'll go with the thought that I'm a pretty good judge of character and if I liked you before my accident then I know I'll like you now. I already do." He gave her his most charming smile. "Besides, if you currently have charge of my grandchildren then I have to place my trust in you."

He let go of her hand and reached for the prosthetic the

hospital had asked her to bring with her.

"Are you allowed up?"

"They gave me crutches and helped me get to the washroom." He pointed to a door near the entrance to the room. "I understand it's important for me to become mobile. Apparently, I can't entertain any thoughts of going home until I can dress myself, go to the bathroom and walk to the end of the hallway and back without assistance."

Margaret watched as he attached his prosthetic leg with expertise and slid into a pair of slippers.

"Will you walk with me?"

"Of course." Her heart skipped a beat at the thought of walking side by side with him once again, even if it was just down the hospital corridor.

He must be comfortable with me. Oh Lord, thank you.

By the time they returned to his room and he to his bed, the signs of physical exhaustion were apparent. His last steps had been wobbly. She helped him turn then lowered the bed so he could easily drop himself onto it. She took his slippers off and assisted with raising his legs and getting him straight on the mattress. He didn't take his eyes off her. When he was settled, he patted the bed for her to sit. She was about to say she should leave so he could rest when he took her hand once again.

"Where are my daughter and son-in-law? I'm assuming I … we were babysitting because they must be away. I understand I was in a coma for a number of days and now awake another twenty-four hours. It seems strange they're not here. Is there a reason?"

Now she wished she had left more quickly. How best to break it to him? He was looking directly at her waiting for an answer.

"Kirsten and Mitchell have been in South America working at a mission, as you have done in the past. When your accident happened, I used your phone to contact them. In their hurry to leave the remoteness to come home and because of low cloud cover, they were forced to take a bus. Along the road, there was an accident and your daughter is in hospital down there."

"Accident? Kirsten's in the hospital? My God, is she badly hurt? What about Mitch? Is he okay?"

"The communication has been poor coming out of Peru. I'm not sure of the extent of Kirsten's injuries and there is still no word on Mitch."

Clarke tightened his grip on her hand. He looked like he was going to faint but before she could call for the nurse, he sat up. "Where's the buzzer? I need to get out of here. I must go home and find out what's going on. You've spoken with Pastor Schmidt? Has anyone contacted the mission people themselves? My God. This has been going on all the while I've been sleeping?"

He stopped his motion suddenly and took Margaret's chin in his hands. "You've had to cope with all this on your own? You're a saint sent from heaven above."

A nurse came through the door just as he was again reaching for his prosthesis.

"Mr. Clarke, where are you going in such a hurry? I just saw you come back from a stroll down the hall. If it's the washroom you need, I'll help you."

"I need my clothes. I'm going home."

"You can't leave. You have at least two more days of strength building before you're well enough to go home."

"I am strong enough. My family need me, now get my clothes. Maggie, see if they're in that closet."

"Clarke, you don't have any clothes here. You came in by ambulance and I took your wet clothes home to launder. I have to get some things for you to wear before you can leave."

"Then you better get them. I am leaving here today."

The nurse rang the buzzer for help. When another nurse came in she was sent to find the doctor.

"Now, Mr. Ingram, please settle down and wait for the doctor to arrive. He needs to sign a release which I doubt he'll do before several tests are done."

Margaret rubbed his arm consolingly. "Let's wait for the doctor. If he says you can go today or tomorrow, I'll bring some clothes for you. Your daughter will need you to be healthy, and so will Kelly and Sean."

Clarke shook his head sadly. "It seems like you have been the strong healthy one. Who has been taking care of you while you've been taking care of everyone and everything else?"

"I just had a reinforcement arrive on the train last evening. She's a good friend and neighbour from my condo building in Ottawa. The children took to her immediately and God only knows what they're up to while I'm here."

Clarke managed a smile.

"What's the cause for all this commotion?" Doctor Kettridge strode through the door.

Chapter Twenty-two

Clarke agreed to wait until evening so further tests could be done. The doctor was adamant about keeping him in for at least another twenty-four hours, but when he realized how agitated his patient became at the thought, he weighed the pros and cons and decided to let the man go home with restrictions. He was to stay in the house and avoid the stairs for two more days. He was also to report to his family doctor within a week. Since his own doctor was seven hundred kilometres away, a follow-up appointment was scheduled for him in Hamilton.

Clarke was startled to learn that Margaret had a legal power-of-attorney for his health care. It seemed to concern him even more that she had the same authority for the children's care.

"I haven't had to use either, Clarke. Kirsten was concerned that no one was legally able to make decisions over your care or her children's while she was in transit and unreachable should the need arise."

"It just makes me feel so vulnerable that my life and those of my grandchildren were placed in the hands of a stranger." No sooner had he said this and the hurt in Margaret's eyes had registered that he obviously regretted his choice of words.

"I'm so sorry. That didn't come out the way it was meant. My daughter has never met you so, in a way, she placed the fate of all of us in your hands, a stranger to her. Forgive me for feeling ... well, helpless."

"Of course. I should have been more thoughtful of your

feelings. I believe the papers state the legality is only in effect as long as you were incapable of making any decisions. We'll have the doctor sign off on that along with your release papers.

"I'll bring the children this evening when I come to take you home. They will be delighted to hear you will be under their roof tonight. Sean always hated leaving you here when visiting hours were over. One morning I found him on your bed at home. He sneaked in during the night because he said he could smell your aftershave on the pillows. I'll let him help me pick out your clothes to bring when we come."

She turned at the door and found he had been watching her while she walked away. He gave a small wave.

❧ ❧ ❧

"What is all this?" Margaret looked at an array of shopping bags and clothing items strewn all over the living room.

"Olivia took us shopping for school clothes. She even bought us new backpacks on wheels." Kelly started foraging through the pile of items. "But I guess if we don't carry them on our backs, we really can't call them backpacks."

"Don't you remember? The store lady called them rolling book bags." Sean spoke with authority.

"Olivia? You spent the morning shopping?"

"On a hot summer day everyone heads for the mall. You know that." She winked at Margaret. "Before you know it, Labour Day will be here and time will have run out to get the best buys."

"We bought something for Grandpa too. We got him a new baseball cap. His other one got ruined when he fell in the pool."

Margaret's eyes brimmed with moisture as she thought of Olivia spending the morning in a mall with two children. Olivia, the glamour girl of their group who shopped only the better stores and boutiques in downtown Ottawa. Olivia, who never had children by her own choice, not that of a higher power.

Olivia, bless her heart, who had jumped on a train and travelled down to help with these children.

"Well, I have a surprise for you, too." The children looked at her empty hands and then to the floor near the entry. "It's not something I bought. It's something that has been given from above. We can pick it up after supper."

Kelly looked like she wanted to say something. "Is it …? is it …? I'm afraid to say it."

Sean blurted out, "Is it Mom and Dad? Are they coming home tonight?"

Kelly was holding her breath.

"It's your grandpa. He's coming home tonight."

Sean gave a whoop. "Hooray! I knew it. I just knew he'd be home soon. Maybe he'll be able to find out what's taking so long with Mom and Dad. Grandpa always knows who to talk to about stuff."

"That's exactly why he wants to come home." Margaret knew he didn't mean she had done less than she could. He was a nine-year-old excited that his grandfather would be here to take care of things. "He wanted to come home this morning but the doctor still had some tests to do so he had to stay until tonight."

Kelly tugged open a bag and pulled out a Hamilton Tiger Cat cap. "We can take this for him to wear home." She remained preoccupied.

"Yeah. Olivia thought we should get him an Ottawa cap because she didn't know he secretly cheers for the Tiger Cats. They were his team before the Red Blacks got started."

"Silly me, what do I know anyway? I thought the Toronto Blue Jays were a hockey team."

"We have to pick all this up and get the house tidied before your grandpa comes home." She motioned to Kelly and Sean. "When you have all your new things put away in your rooms, maybe you can pick out some clothes for your grandpa to wear home from the hospital."

The children set about carrying things to their respective rooms. After a couple of trips back and forth, Kelly approached Margaret in the kitchen.

"I'm happy Grandpa is coming home but I'm happy you've been here to look after us too." Tears welled in her eyes. "I wish my mom was here but since she can't be, you've been just like a grandmother to me. I hope this doesn't mean you are going back to Ottawa. Can you stay for a while?"

"Oh, Kelly. Of course I can. I will stay as long as Clarke wants me to. Come and let me hug you." She put down the bowl she had been wiping and embraced the young girl. "You know I've not been blessed with grandchildren and it's been nice being allowed to be a pretend grandmother even if it's for just a short while. I love you and Sean as if you were my own and it's going to be hard for me to leave."

"Did Grandpa recognize you today?"

"A little bit. He is trying though, and I think with a little time and familiarity, he might remember everything about me soon."

"I hope so. I don't want him to forget you." She gave Margaret an even tighter hug before running off to her room.

Olivia had caught the last part of the conversation. "Was there any progress made in recognition?"

"A little and he's trying. I'm so happy you will get to meet him. He's such a gentleman. I know he's trying really hard to remember what's familiar about me, but he doesn't force it. He's understanding and appreciative that I've been here with the children. All I can do is be here for him."

"You didn't tell us that he has only one leg."

"No. No, I didn't." Margaret hesitated and wiped a spot on a plate over and over again.

"I think that plate is as clean and dry as it's ever going to be."

"I didn't tell you because all of you seemed hung up on his being … well, on being a hunk. Which he's not. Not in the true sense of the word. However, he is as much a man as any six-pack-bearing drop-dead gorgeous man out there. Maybe more so. Instead of developing an outer self, he's been busy developing an inner self that makes anyone who knows him, love him."

"He sounds like quite a man. I will look forward to meeting him." Olivia placed a hand around Margaret's forearm. "I'm sorry if we made you feel defensive. You know we like to tease and this time, unfortunately, you were the target."

Chapter Twenty-three

Sean insisted on pushing his grandfather's wheelchair up the ramp to the front door. Margaret had to give him credit, he did it. At the open door, Olivia greeted them with his canes. Clarke made his way quite steadily to the sliding doors where he insisted on sitting in a chair by the pool.

"This is my favourite place. I find it so tranquil by the water, listening to the waterfall in the little pond."

"I wasn't sure if you might be uncomfortable by the water's edge." Margaret had almost stopped him when first headed in the direction of the patio.

"I don't remember falling in so I have no fear. Maybe tomorrow I won't even be able to look in this direction but for now, I'm enjoying the fresh breeze."

He was wearing his Tiger Cats cap. Sean had been so pleased when Clarke had placed it on his head while still in the hospital gown. His remark "you know how to pick 'em" had put an ear-to-ear grin on the young boy's face.

Margaret had stayed low key and let the children enjoy getting Clarke into the car and taking turns telling him all the latest news, especially about their shopping spree, all the way home. Olivia slipped through the door with a platter of fresh fruit and cheese and placed it on a table near him.

"You must be Olivia, Maggie's friend from Ottawa."

Clarke calling her by the familiar Maggie seemed to slip out naturally.

"Guilty as charged." Olivia placed a napkin on the arm of Clarke's chair and motioned for the children to pass the snacks to him.

"Margaret and I have been neighbours for about eight years. We found a kinship almost immediately and I don't know how she's put up me with for that long but I'm happy she has. I couldn't ask for a better friend."

"You took the train down I understand."

"Yes. I got in about this time yesterday."

"Thank you for doing so. I'm sure it must have been difficult for Maggie to shoulder all of this. My accident was bad enough but to have the responsibility of these two clowns thrown into the fray, it might have been enough to send another person running."

The children giggled when he called them clowns.

"Peggy likes us, Grandpa. She'd never run away." Sean moved closer to sit on a footstool beside his grandfather.

Clarke ruffled the boy's hair. "So let's see these new roller bins you got for school."

"Rolling book bags, Grandpa. They're a new kind of backpack that you pull instead of carrying."

"Well let's have a look at them. And some of those clothes, too."

The kids scrambled inside and Clarke turned to Margaret. "Has there been any news on Kirsten and Mitchell?"

"No. Mr. Wright from the mission keeps in touch but it's never to add anything, only to confirm what they already know and that they are still waiting."

"I'll call an old friend from my mission days. He has a few connections and maybe he can pull a few strings to get something concrete. I'll wait until the children are in bed."

The children performed a fashion show with Grandpa making the appropriate comments and making a joke here and there. Olivia had disappeared into the kitchen and returned later with fresh-baked cupcakes.

"Here's your bed time sugar."

"Mom never lets us have sweets after supper." Sean's eyes were like saucers and he snuck a guilty glance toward Clarke as he took a big bite out of one before anyone could tell him not to.

"What! Did I get that backwards? Is it sugar in the morning and porridge at night?"

"No-o-o." Sean giggled and almost reached for a second cupcake but pulled his hand back when Clarke shot him a disapproving look.

"Mrs. Kovacs is letting you get away with breaking the rules only as a special treat." Clarke smiled at Olivia.

Kelly was quick to interject. "She's not married, Grandpa. She doesn't like us to call her Miss Kovacs either. We have permission to call her Olivia. She's never had a husband and never had children. I'm glad we live here. If we lived in Ottawa, maybe Mom wouldn't have had children either, like Peggy and Olivia."

Both women looked at each other in bewilderment. How astute that Kelly would associate the fact they were both childless and both lived in Ottawa, as if it were something in the air in the northern city.

Clarke caught the discomfort of the women and commented that it was a coincidence that neither woman had children but maybe it was the common feature that had strengthened their friendship. They had each other instead.

He promised to come in and hear their prayers once they were in their pyjamas. Olivia had volunteered to see about their baths and to show Kelly how to wrap her hair so it would be curly in the morning.

When the patio was cleared, Margaret sat in the chair she usually used when she and Clarke were alone in the evening. The crickets were serenading each other and the evening song of the birds could be heard. The sun had just gone down, and the lights reflected in the pool.

"You've been calling me Maggie since you arrived home."

"Isn't that your name?"

"It's what you have called me since we became … friends. You are the only one who uses it."

"I'm sorry. Would you prefer Peggy? Or Margaret? What should I call you?"

She smiled. "You should remain calling me Maggie. It's the name you gave me. I like it when you say it. I consider it almost a term of endearment. I was pleasantly surprised when you used it tonight without any prompting."

"It just slipped out. I didn't even notice. How did the children come to call you Peggy?"

Margaret explained about the Maggie, Meggie, Peggy transition and how they had chosen to use the last version.

"I don't mind. I like that they have a special name for me also."

"They look at you with such admiration and respect."

"They truly are wonderful children and they've made it so easy for me to care for them, and you. The time at the hospital and worrying about their parents can't have been easy for them but they never whined. We just prayed together and accepted the news as we got it. Sean never gave up faith that you would be as good as new in a short time. I've become very fond of them."

Clarke studied her for a few moments. It wasn't uncomfortable. She knew he was trying to remember something, anything familiar.

"Maggie, were we … intimate?"

"No. We were not. Romantic but not intimate."

He started to speak then stopped. He reached for her hand and pulled it to his lips. "I find that so hard to believe."

"You were always a perfect gentleman."

"I was a perfect fool." He laughed and pulled himself up to lean on his canes.

Chapter Twenty-four

"Olivia, I notice some of your things are in the den. Please don't tell me you've been sleeping in there."

"I've only slept one night here and yes, I did use the den. Is that a problem?"

"Not for me it isn't except that I do some of my phone calls from the desk in there. I know that the bedding is fresh in my daughter's room. You would be much more comfortable in there. Plus, you would have your own bathroom."

"Oh, I couldn't. I mean that's their private space."

"From what I can gather I don't think they'll be using their space any time soon. I spoke with the man from the mission and it appears Kirsten's injuries are rather extensive so she can't be moved. Even when we can get her back to Canada, she will be hospitalized for a long time. My son-in-law is still MIA which is not good. Please, I will feel better knowing you're in a comfortable bed. Come, I'll help you move your things."

Once Olivia was ensconced in the master bedroom suite, she told Margaret she was going to luxuriate in the large soaker tub then take a book to bed. It had been a full day for her. The children, while adorable, had worn her out.

Margaret caught up with Clarke in the den where he was trying to make contact with his former friends involved in the missions in South America. So far it had not made international headlines, so they had managed to keep it out of the local news as well. One small bus crash with mostly locals aboard it was not breaking news. They were trying to keep it low profile so that others contemplating volunteering with the missions would not be deterred. Trying to get information out of those involved was like trying to pull teeth.

"Clarke, you must be exhausted. Why don't you call it a night and let me help you get settled into bed?"

"I'm waiting on a phone call from someone whose son is working down there right now. He was going to try to reach him and find out what the word is locally. Sometimes you can learn more from the civilians and natives than you can by going through channels. By the way, did you come across my cell phone anywhere? I usually keep it close to me so it must have been on the patio when I was taken to hospital."

Margaret blushed. "Actually, your cell phone has been my lifeline when I've been at the hospital. Kirsten and I were exchanging conversations on it. I don't own one so it was the children who had presence of mind enough to remember that you would have their parents' phone number on it. It was the only connection I had that first night you were in the emergency ward at the hospital. I've kept it charged and in my purse ever since in case they called."

"I'm glad you were able to make use of it. How smart of those youngsters to remember I had those phone numbers plugged in as contacts. Do you want to keep it for a while?"

"No. You will have more need of it now."

"Did you leave yours in Ottawa?"

She grinned sheepishly. "That's been a bone of contention with my friends for some time now. I don't own one. I refused to be tied down to one. I see everyone always texting and talking on them and I didn't want to be caught in that trap."

"You don't own one? How do you talk to people when you're away from home?"

"I don't."

"You mean I was only able to call you when you were at home?"

"Yes."

He stared at her for a long minute then smiled. "It sounds to me like you are your own person. While I must have found it exasperating, I must say, I admire your tenacity about it."

"I will get yours for you."

She returned minutes later with the phone and charger. "I'll plug it in where you had it. I'll be in my room. Shout when you're ready for me to give you your meds and help you get ready for bed."

"You mean I don't have a bell to ring to bring you running?" He was smiling as he said it, but she thought she detected a slight note of disdain.

"Our relationship wasn't, isn't, like that. You did far more for me than I ever did for you."

"I'm glad to hear that. I would hate to think I took advantage of you. You don't know my daughter and her husband I gather."

"No. They had already left when I came. My visit was kind of an afterthought."

"I missed you." He smiled at her.

"I'd like to think so."

"I very much think you are a woman I would miss."

The phone rang and Clarke picked it up. "Yes, Bernard, I'm here. What have you found out?"

Margaret left the room and went downstairs to get into her pyjamas. When she returned a half hour later, Clarke was deep in thought.

"Was he able to help you?"

"I'm not sure. He said that as far as they can tell, the bus driver, Mitchell, and an American have all disappeared. It looks like they may have left the scene together."

"What are you saying?"

"I don't know quite what to make of it. He wasn't sure if they may have left to get help and then got lost or if they fled the scene. Rumours are rampant about a number of possibilities. Some think he may have been kidnapped by the driver and the American. Some say he and the driver did the kidnapping and the American was the victim. Others think all three may have been hi-jacked and taken for ransom by some drug dealers who have been stopping traffic on that road."

"Does Mitchell have money? Kidnappers usually target wealthy victims who can pay a high ransom. It looks to me like he and Kirsten live comfortably but not extravagantly."

"This adds a whole new layer to this *accident* which resulted in my daughter suffering life-threatening injuries. Tomorrow, I will be in touch with our embassy down there. We must get her safely away from there and back on Canadian soil. Then we'll deal with the whereabouts of Mitchell."

Margaret put her hand on Clarke's shoulder. "My poor darling, I wish I could have spared you this. I was hoping by the time you woke from your coma that Kirsten and Mitchell would be home and all would be well. Instead …"

"Instead I woke up to find I have a beautiful girlfriend who has been doing a marvelous job caring for my grandchildren who, in turn, are dealing with the fact their parents may not be home for a long time. How lucky I am to have you in my life."

"Clarke, I —"

"Shhh. Don't say anything. I think I need to lie down now then take a fresh look at all of this in the morning."

She helped Clarke into his room and laid out clean pyjamas for him. She waited while he took care of his nighttime ritual in the bathroom. She helped him ease his prosthesis off, and folded the sheets back so all he had to do was slip his pyjamas on and pull the covers up.

"I'll bring your meds and water and put them on your night

table. Can I get you anything from the kitchen?"

"No. I'll be fine, thank you."

It was nearing midnight and she knew he must be exhausted. She switched the lights off and checked the door locks before returning to his room with his medication. He was under the covers and checking his phone when she walked in. He patted the bed for her to sit.

"How did we meet?"

"It was in the natural supplements section of the drug store in our neighbourhood in Ottawa. You saw me reading labels and offered some advice."

"Doesn't sound very romantic."

"It wasn't but your kind manner and patient concern touched me. My friends always accused me of being a hypochondriac and I was relieved when you seemed genuinely interested in what I was saying."

"Are you a hypochondriac?"

"No. Well, maybe. Yes, I guess I was, back then."

"But you're not anymore?"

"No. I haven't had an ache, pain or indigestion since I met you."

"What do you attribute that to?"

"You gave me other things to think about besides myself.'

"Like what?"

"Like going to the museums. Watching old movies at the Lyceum. Lunches and dinners out. Walking in the parks around the city. Visiting new out-of-the-way restaurants."

"Now that sounds more interesting."

"Much more."

"Is the drug store the one at the end of Windsor Street?"

"Yes."

"And we went to all those places. It sounds like you brought me out of my shell."

"You were in a shell?"

"I never really had any interest in women after my wife died. I guess I didn't think any would be interested in me."

"You never gave me any indication of being shy or reclusive. You were very outgoing and made the first overtures in our relationship. We've shared many laughs, many wonderful hours together."

"I feel comfortable with you, like I know you. I just can't seem to remember all of this. I want to remember all these great times, too, Maggie. I don't want any of our firsts to be kept from me." He brushed her cheek with the back of his hand then pulled her in to kiss her forehead. "Good night, sweet lady. Those children will have us up early no doubt."

Chapter Twenty-five

Clarke was growing more frustrated by the hour. He was stonewalled in every direction. No one had answers for him. Those he did receive were contradictory to each other: the embassy, agencies, personal contacts. Margaret watched his desperation grow as each phone call proved fruitless.

He had spent an hour with the children with promises of a trip to a Ti-Cat's home game in the near future. Olivia, sensing Clarke's need for privacy and discretion in front of the children during his attempts at bringing his daughter and son-in-law home, offered to take them and two of their friends to Adventure Village on the beach of Lake Ontario. She had already rented a vehicle for a week, her original guess at a time frame for staying. It had proved a wise decision to take a SUV since it looked like she was going to be the surrogate grandmother for the next few days — at least until Clarke had done whatever he could to overcome the challenges at hand. Olivia became defensive at Margaret's raised eyebrow when she offered to keep the children busy for them. "I don't know why you are so surprised. I was a kid once you know. I can handle this."

"But four at once?"

"Bringing friends along will keep them busy. They're not toddlers that need their bums wiped or fed their soup by spoon. They'll entertain each other. All I have to do is supervise. Besides, they don't need to hear all the bad news coming, or not coming, out of Peru. If I can give them a day of respite from missing their parents, it's the least I can do for the poor kids."

She and her carload of excited children planned to leave in good time to do some rock climbing and get in a round of mini-golf before the mid-to-late-afternoon traffic developed.

Margaret teared up and raised her eyes once again in thanksgiving for the friendship of such a generous, caring woman.

"But if you have any thoughts of ruining my image by telling the others I spent a whole day with a van load of screaming pre-teens, I'll tell them how you struggle into a girdle every day."

"I don't!"

"They won't know that." She closed the door and ushered the waiting children into the van. "Don't wait supper for us."

"She's right, you know."

Margaret hadn't heard Clarke wheel up behind her. "Those kids don't need to watch me becoming more frustrated by the hour. They need some laughter and time with their friends. You could and should have gone also."

He looked fragile with his slender frame and dark-circled eyes. "I am needed here. I want to be here." She patted his shoulder as she walked past him.

"I'll make fresh coffee for you. Do you want a cupcake?"

"I'll take both out on the patio, since you're offering."

He told her about the non-progress he had made. "I've heard stories of people who have lost family members in various places of South America. Sons, husbands, daughters, fathers who have been missing for years with no answers as to their whereabouts. I always thought they must not be trying hard enough. This is the twenty-first century after all. With all the communication satellites, modes of transportation, government agencies and foreign services available, no one can just disappear. Apparently, I've been wrong."

He had moved onto a patio sofa and motioned for Margaret

to sit beside him. "I've been down there a number of times and have never felt unsafe. If I had, I would have argued strongly against my daughter going down to do as I had done. There are always mission officials, other workers, locals, women and children, and government workers around. It's a village atmosphere where everyone appreciates the others' work, the others' company."

He took Margaret's hand and interlaced their fingers. "God-help me, I'm so angry that these volunteers can be treated so badly. It's as if no one cares about them. Here's a woman who has a family, two young children that need her at home thousands of miles away. If for no other reason, you would think they'd be anxious to be rid of the expense of nursing her wounds. They should have had her on a plane back to Canada days ago."

She let him rant. He needed to release this pent-up anger and anxiety and she was willing to be the listener.

"I can't find anyone who can tell me exactly what her injuries are. The mission assures me she is covered by their insurance. Someone from the embassy has contacted the hospital only to learn she is in surgery each time they call. I have trouble finding anyone who speaks English and my Spanish is not great. If I can just get her home and in a hospital here, then I can concentrate on finding Mitchell."

"Have you talked to his sister?"

"Yes. She is concerned for his safety and asked to be kept informed."

"Is she asking any questions? Doing any searching herself?"

"I understand she left home at a young age and that she and Mitch are not close. I doubt we'll get much assistance or support from her."

He turned to Margaret. She sat while he looked at her eyes, her hair, her mouth and back to her eyes again.

"I'm so sorry you've been forced to suffer through all this

turmoil. Me. The children. My daughter. You could be at home enjoying whatever it is you do in Ottawa."

He leaned back as if to get a good view of her. "What is it you do in Ottawa?"

"I play bridge."

"That's it? You play bridge."

"I told you I was very self-centred and so bored as to imagine aches and pains."

"I'll bet you're the best bridge player in the city. You strike me as a woman who would be the best at whatever you do."

Margaret laughed. "I'm a good bridge player, a good cook, a good friend, a good person. The endearing qualities of a loyal dog with the addition of being able to count trump cards and put a meal on the table instead of waiting to be fed."

"I think you're a far more desirable companion than a dog for many reasons, Maggie. I'm learning how easy it must have been for me to fall in love with you."

The conversation was interrupted by the phone. Margaret ran into the kitchen to answer it.

"Clarke, it's Malcolm Wright from the Mission."

She handed him the phone and was about to leave when he grasped her wrist and asked her stay.

Someone from the Mission staff in Lima had gone directly to the hospital and demanded answers. It appeared that Kirsten had suffered numerous fractures to various areas of her body as well as a large amount of blood loss. She was in an out of consciousness and was showing signs of developing infection. Transporting her back to Canada was out of the question until she could be stabilized enough to travel. She was not out of the woods and needed twenty-four-hour care in the intensive care unit of the hospital. It might be another week before they could consider air transport home then many months of future surgeries and recuperation in hospital. Malcolm was going to stay in constant contact with the Mission in Lima and would update Clarke as he heard more.

Margaret could hear the beeping sounds of the disconnected line as Clarke continued to stare at it. She noticed a drop of moisture fall on the receiver and sat down beside her gentle, hurting man and slid her arms around his waist. He gently pressed her head against his shoulder while he kissed the top of her head.

"Thank you for being in my life."

Chapter Twenty-six

"Do you know there's a pervert living on this street?"

Margaret choked on a bite of cupcake. "What are you talking about?"

"The kids were talking about it today."

"What? They know about him and he's not been arrested?"

"All I know is, he lives in the blue house, second from the corner. I think everyone spends too much time in their backyards when they should be watching what's going on out front."

"What did the children say about him? Are they frightened?"

"It seems one of the friends heard his mother and father talking about him. The boy's father told his mother to be careful of him and not to let him in the house."

"Really! I'll have to ask Clarke if he knows of him and if the children should be warned."

"I guess they already know because the other young girl said her dad hates the guy too and even said he should be locked up."

"Maybe he's already on an offenders' list. I'll talk to Clarke about it. Chances are he doesn't even know about the man."

"Just make sure your front door is always locked and don't let the children answer the doorbell."

Clarke was in the den with the children listening to a detailed report of the day's adventures. The women walked in just in time to hear Sean describing Olivia's mini-golf skills.

"She's good, Grandpa. She beat an old guy by six strokes."

Margaret turned to Olivia. "Beating up on old men now, are you?"

"It's not my fault he didn't know how to use his putter. I should have known by his argyle socks that he wasn't into sports."

"What's argyle?" Kelly looked confused.

"If you look in my bedroom dresser you'll see several pairs." Clarke's amusement showed in his eyes.

"Sorry, Clarke, but I can't take back my feelings about those socks being dated."

"But I only wear them with my knickers."

"Where did you say you found this dinosaur, Margaret?" Olivia gave Clarke a pat on the shoulder as she said it.

"Did dinosaurs wear argyle, Grandpa?" Now Sean was confused also.

"No, honey. Olivia is just being funny about old men who wear outdated styles. She doesn't appreciate those of us who know some fashions are classic and never go out of style." He slipped Olivia a grin before asking about the rock climbing the children had enjoyed.

"It was real fun. Olivia was disappointed they wouldn't let her climb, too. Sean really wanted her to because he wanted to race her to the top. I think they would have let her if she didn't have a pacemaker on her heart. They said they have safety guidelines they have to follow. I think it was good they didn't let her because what if she fell and her pacemaker broke?"

"Pacemaker? Really, Olivia!"

Margaret couldn't believe her ears. This is the Olivia that refuses to dine out in family restaurants because of the noise. The same Olivia who goes to adults-only beauty salons and goes to the late showing at movie theatres to ensure no children ruin her enjoyment of the film.

"Well, well, well. Tell us more." She sat on the floor beside

Kelly. "What else did Olivia do that us older folks might not ask to do?"

"That's about all we had time for, but she did promise to go on the bungee trampoline if she comes back again. It looked like loads of fun."

"And it doesn't let you bounce higher than four storeys so there's no harm whatsoever." Olivia rolled her eyes.

Clarke shook his head. "You're a good sport."

"Grandpa did you get any more news about Mom and Dad?" Kelly brought them back to reality with that one simple question.

"Yes, I did. Mr. Wright called me with some news." He stopped to take a couple of deep breaths. "Your mother has some serious injuries that need to heal somewhat before she can take that long plane ride home. She is in an excellent hospital in Lima, Peru. You can find where that is on your globe. It's in the same part of South America in which they were working but it's a big modern city. When she has recovered enough to travel she will come home and spend the rest of her recovery time in a hospital here."

"Can we phone her?"

"Is Daddy there too? Is he okay?"

"Can we go visit her?"

"Whoa. One question at a time." He held his hands up as if fending them off. "No, we can't phone her. She is sleeping most of the time and when she's awake she's busy with the doctors and nurses. She needs her sleep to heal so we don't want to wake her up and slow down the healing process."

Margaret wondered how Clarke was going to handle the questions about Mitchell. He had dodged that question easily with the children being distracted.

"I wasn't able to learn anything new about your dad. Maybe he's in a smaller hospital and has no identification on him. Maybe he's being cared for in a private home and has a little bit of amnesia like me. In any event he hasn't been identified yet and that's a good thing because they have the names of the people who died in the crash. Your dad is not one of them. We'll just keep praying that he's not injured too badly and that he's getting good care. Maybe he's busy looking for your mother. We'll find out soon, I hope." He reached for his wheelchair. "Now, last one in the pool has to cook breakfast tomorrow. Go put your swimsuits on."

Predictably, it was Clarke who was last in. The children were cannonballing into foam noodle rings. Margaret and Olivia were floating on slices of rubber watermelon and all was well with the world.

Chapter Twenty-seven

"I guess you will be staying in Hamilton for the foreseeable future."

Clarke was sitting on the patio in his bathrobe when Olivia brought out three glasses of wine on a tray.

"I've been running several scenarios through my head since I spoke with Malcolm. I'm not sure what to do."

"What alternatives are there?"

Clarke shrugged his shoulders. "None that are great."

Olivia stood and watched the lights in the water.

"This is such a lovely backyard. It's so private and peaceful. Sitting here makes me feel like I'm in a forest with no neighbours for miles. It's hard to believe a city is just on the other side of that fence. I'll have a hard time leaving and going back to Ottawa in a few days."

"Must you leave? Why not extend your visit for another week or so?"

"That's kind of you but I have a couple of appointments next week, one in particular that can't be postponed. Besides I think you and Margaret could use some alone time to become reacquainted."

"I really appreciated your dropping everything to come and give me your support, Olivia. You have no idea how much I valued your help." Margaret smiled at her friend.

"And I appreciate the time you've spent with the children the last couple of days. It has certainly given me some time to try and get matters cleared up in South America without them over-hearing conversations they needn't know about. It can't have been easy entertaining not only my two but the neighbour's children as well. You're a wonder woman. Thank you from the bottom of my heart. Both of you." His sweeping glance took in Margaret as well.

"I guess you'll be staying for a little while?" Olivia looked at her friend.

"If Clarke will have me, I thought I would stay at least until he's a little stronger and maybe until something definite is in the works for Kirsten's return."

"Clarke would be devastated if you left anytime soon." He answered in the third person then continued. "I am hoping you will stay with me for a long while yet." He reached for her hand.

"On that note, I am going to bed. I can't remember ever spending a more exhilarating day and I'm about done in. Thank God my pacemaker kept me from climbing that wall."

"Exhilarating isn't the word I would have used. You are being kind and I and the children love you for it. Good night, Olivia." Clarke rose and gave her a kiss on the cheek.

Olivia winked at Margaret and whispered, "Don't you dare leave this man anytime soon."

Clarke lifted his artificial leg onto a wicker ottoman and sipped his wine.

"I'm hoping you don't have to rush back to Ottawa, Maggie."

"I can't stay indefinitely. My friends can look after my place for a while longer but sooner or later, I have to take care of some things. I have a kitchen renovation scheduled for September and I still have appliances to purchase and flooring, cupboards, countertops, and so on to choose. My annual physical check-up and mammogram are approaching. These are things I can't do from a distance. What about you? Is your place okay for an indefinite stay here?"

"My condo is okay, but I checked my appointment schedule on my computer and I have doctors' appointments also. I've come to rely on the doctors who have been taking care of me all these years. I'm glad I woke up before I was transferred to a long-term care here. I would have preferred to go home. That's why I was contemplating possible alternatives. I only hope I can get answers about Kirsten soon. If I was healthy, I would fly down and try to speed things up from that end. I want to hold my daughter and give her a big bear hug and kiss away her hurts like I used to when she was a little girl. I doubt I could get travel insurance after just being released from the hospital and suffering some kind of brain trauma. The school year will be starting soon also. I have a responsibility to get the children enrolled and into their classes."

"I think there are no possible alternatives for you but to wait until Kirsten can come home. By the sound of things, it may not be until after school starts."

"I know. If Mitch isn't found, I will have to arrange for Kirsten's long-term care which means me moving permanently down here or having her brought directly to an Ottawa hospital."

"And the children? What about school?"

"Aye, there's the rub. I know they can be enrolled in school in Ottawa, but a downtown condo is no place to raise children. They need a yard and space to play. There is nothing to do, I guess, until Kirsten can come home, or Mitch is found. What do you think?"

She took several deep breaths, mulling his words over carefully. It certainly was a conundrum. The poor man was not well himself and now had all this responsibility thrown at him.

"If Mitchell doesn't show up by the time Kirsten is well enough to travel, it makes a lot of sense to have her flown directly to Ottawa General. The hardest part would be uprooting the children from their friends and classmates. But take a look at the yard here. The amount of play space is almost nil. It's all swimming pool which can only be used a few months of the year. They could adapt to condo living and Ottawa is teaming with fresh air activity for young people, however they would only have you. Possibly their mother — if she heals well. It might only be for a year then they could move back home. It would mean you can live in your own home, see your own doctors and therapists. Your memory might return quicker in a familiar place. You can oversee every aspect of Kirsten's care and recovery programs.

"I don't know what to say about their home sitting vacant. I don't think it should be sold in case six months or a year from now Kirsten is well enough to move back and continue to raise the children in Hamilton, with or without a husband."

"You have some valid points, Maggie. I suppose I could have a property management firm look after renting this house out short term. I just wish we knew where my son-in-law is. It's not looking good if they can find no trace of him. He is not the type to just disappear and I don't believe for one minute that he's involved in anything illegal. My fear is that if he's not already dead he soon will be. Kidnap victims down there are not usually found alive." He wiped his forehead with a tissue. "I can't help dreading what my poor daughter is facing when she wakes up. This time her daddy can't make it all go away."

The tears came then. He sobbed so hard his whole body shook. After holding him for a long while, Margaret managed to get him into bed and brought his meds with a glass of water.

"You get some sleep, my darling. You woke up in the hospital and found yourself in the middle of a huge mess and your body still needs to heal. Tomorrow may bring good news and answers will be found."

"Lay with me, Maggie. I just need to feel you next to me."

She stretched out beside him on the bed and rested a hand on his shoulder. "I'll help you through it, my love."

He laid his hand over hers. "I had been determined to be independent, not to be a burden on anyone for so many years I guess I forgot how to ask for help. It feels good to have someone to talk things over with."

"You are not a burden. But we all are given burdens we must carry from time to time and we'll carry this one together if you let me help." She kissed his shoulder and fell asleep listening to his breathing.

Chapter Twenty-eight

It was almost dawn when she was awakened by the sound of sobbing. She followed the sound to her own room and found Kristen sitting on the floor beside her bed, crying.

"Sweetie, what's wrong?" She sat on the floor beside the girl.

"I woke up and started thinking about my mother and needed to talk to you but you weren't here. I looked in the kitchen and the den but you weren't anywhere. I … I … thought you left but just now I saw that your stuff's still here."

Margaret put her arms around the girl. "I would never leave without saying goodbye."

"You aren't, are you? Leaving that is? Olivia said she will be going home in a few more days. I wish she didn't have to. I hope you won't go home for a long time."

"I'm not going anywhere for a while. Eventually, I will have to. My apartment is being renovated next month and I have to be there. I also have some appointments I have to keep but by then you'll be in school and most likely your mother will be home."

"Do think she'll really be home by then?"

"I can't promise anything I'm not one hundred percent sure about, but I think the chances are pretty good."

"Where were you just now?"

"Your grandpa wasn't feeling very good either. He's worried about your mother, too. I had to go and sit with him for a little while until he fell asleep. Dear me, I think we all need a good holding-hands-sitting-around-a-bonfire comfort session."

"Grandpa's going to be okay though, isn't he?"

"Clarke has been so strong and gotten so many things done in the single day he's been home that we forget he just got out of the hospital himself. He still needs tender loving care. I think tomorrow we should make him a nice big banana cream pie."

Kelly's eyes lit up. "Did you know that's his absolute favourite?"

"I did."

"Why do you think he doesn't remember you?"

"I don't know, dear. Maybe that part of his brain was without oxygen for just a moment too long. It needs a wee bit longer to repair itself and fix his rememberer."

"I can see he still likes you."

"Can you? I think he still does too. He just needs time to remember it also."

"Does it bother you?"

"It does a little, but I know it's not his fault. He's trying very hard. Now why don't you try to get just another hour or two of sleep and we'll think really hard of something nice to do for Olivia tomorrow, too."

"She's really nice and so funny. Jamie and Sonya thought so too. She made us laugh lots."

After Kelly was tucked back into bed, Margaret slid between the sheets on her own bed and closed her eyes. "Please, dear God, give this poor family a break. Clarke deserves to get his daughter back soon and ditto for those poor children. They are such a close-knit, full of faith family. Please bring them all together again. I don't know what the story is with their father, but he must be a man of faith also. This is not the first year he has served in your name down there. I'm not asking for myself. I don't deserve any favours but they do. I don't like to tell you how to do things, God, but the sooner you can bring them home the better. Amen."

❣ ❣ ❣

The shriek of the smoke alarm had Margaret out of bed and up the stairs in darn near zero seconds. In the kitchen were two frightened children standing in front of a smoking oven. Clarke was quick to respond also, moving quickly on one leg and crutches, hair all askew.

"We were going to surprise you with fresh baked muffins." Sean's words were hardly distinguishable amidst the bawling.

"We wanted to do something nice for everyone but we … we … goofed. Sorta." Kelly threw the oven mitts on the floor and threw herself into Margaret's arms.

Clarke opened the patio doors to let the smoke out then pulled a muffin tray out of the oven. They had been filled too full and the batter had overflowed onto the red-hot bottom element. Outside of an oven that would need cleaning, the only damage done was the loss of a dozen muffins.

"We helped Mom make them a few times, but I guess we never watched how much batter she put in the tins. Grandpa, I'm really sorry." Kelly's eyes were brimming with unshed tears. "Everybody is tired from looking after us and we wanted to do something for you. We wanted you to wake up and see the surprise."

Sean was still sobbing.

Olivia finally wandered into the room with earplugs in her hand and a black sleeping mask on top of her head like a pair of raised sunglasses. "What the heck is going on?"

Everyone looked from one to another and suddenly the room was full of adult laughter.

"You're not mad at us?" Sean hiccupped as he tried to stop crying.

"No, son. We're not mad, just glad it's no worse than a few burnt muffins."

"I could use a cup of coffee. C'mon kids. Let's go pick up some muffins at Tim Horton's. I'll put my housecoat on. Margaret, you and Clarke have the coffee ready when we get back." She disappeared down the hall, reappearing a minute later wearing a sleeveless long dress. She rattled the car keys and went out the front door, kids following in the T-shirts and track pants they had slept in.

Clarke looked at Margaret. "Please tell me the day will go uphill from here."

She smiled. "We could get a call that Olivia made a wrong turn and they're in Burlington."

He leaned against the cupboard. "She saved the day. Those kids were devastated that their surprise ended in disaster. Olivia didn't hesitate. She gave them no time dwell on it and made an adventure out of it. What remarkable women you are. Are the others the same?"

"You'd think we were sisters in blood."

"That's it. I have to seriously think of taking this show to Ottawa. I can see it's going to take a village. I will never do it alone."

She felt him watching her most of the morning. He seemed mesmerized.

Margaret, Olivia and the children played scrabble after they ate their muffins. The four of them also sat in front of the computer while Kelly Googled everything she could find on Peru, including Lima hospitals. When she was satisfied that they looked modern, she then zeroed in on the territory where her parents had been working. She showed her brother and the women the hills and valleys and some of the steep mountain terrain.

"Do you really think my dad is lost?"

"Don't you?" Margaret asked.

"I don't know. I don't even know what the best thing is that could have happened to him. Sometimes I hope he's in a hospital somewhere but then I know he'd be very badly hurt if he wasn't able to tell them who he is and how to reach us. Then I wonder if he bumped his head, too, and maybe he's wandering around in the jungle not knowing where he is. That would be awful. You don't think he was kidnapped, do you?" The earnestness in her voice was heartbreaking.

Olivia spoke up. "Honey, you can drive yourself crazy imagining things. Just remember that he is somewhere and wherever that somewhere is, he is alive and well and worried knowing that you are doing exactly this, imagining all kinds of terrible situations. Don't forget, he went down to work for God and maybe somebody he has helped is now helping him. Maybe he can't get out of wherever he is, but as soon as he can, he'll come home just as quick as an airplane can bring him."

Sean was deep in thought.

"Daddy told me one time when we were out hiking that if I ever got lost, I should stay right where I am until somebody finds me. He said the worst thing I could do is try to find my way out because I could be moving farther and farther away from help. I think that's what he's doing. He's staying where he is until somebody finds him. What do you think, Peggy?"

"I think your father is a very smart man. He knows exactly what to do. It may take a little while, but they'll find him because he knows to stay put."

Kelly closed the lid on the computer. "May I go to Sonya's house for a while? She wants to show me her new school outfits."

"Watch out for that pervert." Sean sounded alarmed.

Clarke had just entered the den. "What pervert?"

Olivia told him about the conversation in the car from the day before.

"Kelly, best you don't leave the house until I get to the

bottom of this."

He looked up a number and dialled. They listened to his end of the conversation and were surprised when he started to laugh. They were waiting with open mouths when he cut the connection.

"Kelly, you can go on over to Sonya's. There is no pervert. At least not in the strict sense of the word. Sean, you can play games in your room while I explain to the women. There's nothing to worry about."

"It ended up being a couple of jealous husbands. A single man recently moved into the neighbourhood. Apparently, he's a fitness freak and likes to flaunt his well-muscled body by mowing the lawn shirtless. Of course the women who live close by made a habit of weeding their flower gardens or at least watching from their windows on his lawn-grooming days. It only took a few comments and a couple lewd remarks before the husbands started referring to him as a pervert. At a recent barbecue, the men started joking about locking their wives and daughters up when the pervie's outside. Children being children misconstrued the humour for fact and the story grew."

"The poor guy is probably wondering why the guys in the hood don't talk to him. Someone should invite him over for a beer. They might find out he's one nice guy."

"You're right, Olivia. We shouldn't judge. The guy got labelled just because he's got a few muscles."

Margaret couldn't help thinking that she and her friends probably would have labelled him a hunk.

Chapter Twenty-nine

"Why don't you ladies take the afternoon to do something together?"

Margaret and Olivia looked at each other. Both reacted at the same time.

"But what would we do?"

"I can't think of anywhere I want to go."

Clarke laughed. "You sound like a couple of bored kids saying there's nothing to do. Surely, after the last hectic week and rather eventful morning, there must be some quiet place, with no demands, no kids, nobody calling you where you might take refuge for a while. A spa? A movie? A museum? A walk along a beach?"

"I don't know about you, Margaret, but I can beach out by the pool here as well as anywhere."

"I'm with you. A good book, a glass of iced tea, some soft music and I'd be in heaven."

"The kids might not be quiet for long." Clarke seemed disappointed by their decision.

"Are you trying to get rid of us?" Olivia put her hands on her hips. "You can tell them the pool is off limits — adults only day today."

"Suit yourself."

The two women moved the pool chairs to the shade and set their glasses on the small table between them.

"Ahhh, it will be nice to finally get into one of the books I brought."

"You've had a long stretch of stress, Margaret. You've held up well. Two days and I'm done in." Olivia took a long sip of her cold drink.

"You forget, you've been more active than I. Entertaining four ten-year-olds at an amusement park is more than I could ever dream of doing."

"Yes. That was kind of nutso. But, you know, Margaret? It was fun and I felt like I was *doing* something. Really *doing* something. I get to wondering what life is all about sometimes. Bridge, beauty salon, spa, the theatre, then bridge, beauty salon, and so on and so on. The last two days I felt needed, useful." She flipped on to her side and reached for Margaret's hand. "You are so lucky. You have a whole new life with Clarke and the children. Did I tell you that Kelly asked if I thought you would mind her calling you Grandma?"

"She did?"

"Yes, she did. Those kids love you, Margaret. And Clarke may not remember who you are but if someone looked at me the way he looks at you, I'd be licking his boots. He can't keep his eyes off you."

She sat up. "On that subject, why the hell did we never meet him? You shut us right out."

Margaret blushed. "I guess I was worried you girls might not accept him, accept us. You all seem so consumed with men being hunks that I wondered if you would disapprove of a man who isn't. A hunk that is."

"Clarke may not be big and muscular, but he is one of the sexiest men I've ever met. I can't believe you think we are that shallow. I'm hurt. Margaret, I hope you're not ashamed or embarrassed that he is handicapped."

"Of course, I'm not ashamed of him. I love him deeply. I did almost from the very start. I am sorry because I did doubt his acceptance by you girls. I was stressed because I wanted him to be a part of my life, but I was worried it might be at the cost of the friendship of my friends. It's not that I think you shallow, I just know that appearance is important to all of you."

"Margaret, Margaret. Appearance is everything. Clean, well-groomed, fashionably dressed, not nerdy. Heh, heh, sounds like I'm describing a job applicant. I just mean I hate any man who goes around unshaven, a hairy belly-button sticking out under a T-shirt with printing on the front and back, no deodorant and … and … dirty hair and uncut toenails. Those types usually end up calling you 'doll' or 'babe' and expect you to keep the beer cold."

Margaret laughed. "You are describing a lot of men whose significant others find them very attractive. I get what you are saying though — he doesn't necessarily have to be built like The Rock, he just has to be clean, genteel. We are all drawn to different types, thank goodness. Life would be a bitch if we were all seeking the same person. The same can be said in reverse. I'm glad all men aren't searching for Raquel Welch or there would be a lot of lonely women running around out there, including me."

"Helen and Sarah can hardly wait to meet him."

"You've been talking to them?"

"I called each of them last night before I fell asleep. I'm surprised one or both didn't phone you. They think I'm exaggerating about spending the day with a bunch of children."

"Did you tell them you promised to go bungee jumping?"

"Are you nuts? Helen has my power-of-attorney. I'm afraid she'd think I was off my rocker and act on it. Besides it's not bungee jumping, it's bungee trampoline. There's a subtle difference." She took another long drink. "So, what happens now?"

"Clarke is facing a real dilemma. Poor guy. He should be relaxing and letting his brain heal. Instead, he's trying to get his daughter back home. Language and culture barriers, distance, remoteness are all hampering that process. He has grandchildren to enroll in school, a son-in-law to find. He wants to go home but feels compelled to stay here. It sounds like his daughter could be in for an extremely long recovery period with multiple surgeries along the way. He would prefer that take place in Ottawa where he needs care by his own doctors but … the children and the husband."

"What do you want, Margaret?"

"I want to be with him, wherever that is. I would prefer Ottawa but have to respect whatever choice he makes." Her voice quivered. "The poor man has to remember me. He has to know he can trust me. I can't imagine being inside his head right now."

"This may sound corny but I envy you. I wish I had someone who needs me the way Clarke needs you. I don't mean just *anyone* who can help him. He needs *you*. He needs you to love him and he needs to love you in return. That's what will keep him going, what will give this difficult journey a purpose. I don't think it matters as much to him as it does to you that he doesn't remember your history. I can see he likes what he knows and feels in the present, in the now. You are the genuine article, Margaret, and he senses it. You are one lucky woman to have found this man, and he you."

Chapter Thirty

Clarke kept the children occupied until suppertime. The women spent little time reading, their afternoon was filled mostly by napping and talking. Margaret had quietly mulled over Olivia's words and observations, wishing she had access to Clarke's mind and what he was thinking deep down within.

By unanimous agreement the decision was made to go out for supper. Clarke was familiar with an oyster bar situated in the unlikely flatlands on the northern outskirts of Burlington, across the bridge from Hamilton. All of them fit comfortably in Olivia's rental SUV. The menu was expansive enough to please everyone's tastes. A stop at Hutch's Ice Cream Parlour on the way home finished the evening exactly to the children's liking.

"A pleasant ending to a day that started rather hectically." Olivia parked the vehicle back in the driveway and unlocked the doors to let her passengers out.

"I liked the ice cream the best." Sean stroked his tummy in obvious delight.

"What? You didn't like the slithery, slimy oysters?" Clarke teased him.

"Yuck, Grandpa. I even hated the way they smelled."

"Next time maybe we can go straight to Hutch's and just have hot dogs and ice cream?" Kelly suggested hopefully.

"Or next time we can get a babysitter and go ourselves." Clarke patted Sean on the bum. "Now, you two get ready for bed. We have some talking and planning to do tomorrow."

When Margaret went into Kelly's room later to say good night, she found the girl a little disturbed.

"Are you angry with Sean and me?"

"Angry? About what?"

"That we made a mess in the kitchen and almost set the house on fire this morning?"

Margaret sat on the girl's bed. "Oh, honey, why would I be angry about your trying to make such a nice surprise for us? What happened was an accident that could have happened to anyone. I don't think the house was about to catch on fire, either. The worst that might have happened was the house may have filled with smoke from the burnt batter."

"But we were supposed to make Grandpa a banana cream pie and we didn't. He told us to let you and Olivia have some time alone so he kept us away from the pool and patio. I thought it was because you were mad at me."

"Sweetie, making the pie slipped my mind after all the morning's activity. This afternoon, your grandpa thought Olivia and I needed some time to spend just with each other. She came all this way and we hadn't really had a chance to visit. That's all there was to it. We can try to find time to make the pie tomorrow. Now you sleep well and dream about ice cream cones and bananas dancing on top of a nice thick cream pie."

She kissed the girl's forehead and was about to leave the room when Kelly grasped her arm. "Peggy?"

"Yes, dear?"

"Do you think maybe I could change your name one more time?" Her voice sounded hesitant.

"To what? I hope nothing with Crabby or Old in it."

"No. I wondered if I could call you Grandma." She pulled the covers over her face as quickly as the words were spoken.

Margaret stared at the sheet covering the sweet, hurting little girl. She could feel a twinge in her own heart. The thought of being called Grandma had disappeared from her dreams several decades ago. Now she was being offered this treasured gift by a child she would dearly love to have for a grandchild. She sat back on the bed and gently tugged at the sheet.

"I am so touched that you can even think of me as a grandma."

"I can't help it. I wish you were my grandma. Maybe you and Grandpa can get married and then you really will be."

"Oh, honey. I can't think of anything nicer than being your grandma. However, I'm not sure that your grandpa is quite ready for a big change like that." She noticed Kelly bunching the sheet into her fist.

"Why don't we wait until your mother comes home and you can discuss the name change with her? In the meantime, you can keep my love in your heart just as if I was your grandmother and I will keep yours."

Kelly reluctantly agreed.

Margaret felt she had dodged a bullet and hoped she had bought some time. She had no idea where the relationship between her and Clarke was headed and that poor little girl didn't need to find a grandmother only to lose her.

Olivia had retired to her bedroom suite so Margaret wandered into the kitchen to make sure the ingredients were at hand for banana cream pie. Clarke was sitting on a stool with the newspaper open on the island's granite countertop. He looked up as she neared. His eyes held a strange look, almost brooding.

"Are you in pain, Clarke?" She glanced down and saw he was wearing his prosthetic.

"No. I'm fine."

"I just tucked Kelly into bed. She was worried that I was angry with her and Sean after this morning's little fiasco."

He didn't answer, just continued watching her as she moved from cupboard to cupboard.

"She thought Olivia and I had purposely isolated ourselves from them on the patio all afternoon."

"She didn't say anything to me."

"You're not the one she felt was angry. Not having had a lot of experience with children I sometimes have trouble picking up signals. I would hate if I did anything to make the children doubt my feelings for them."

"What are your feelings for them?"

She sighed. "I'm coming to care for them very deeply. They're … they're…" She didn't want to admit grandmotherly feelings.

"They're such good kids."

He turned on the stool and took Margaret's hand when she set measuring cups and spoons on the counter.

"I have a feeling you started to say something else."

Startled, her eyes moved from where his hand was placed on hers to look directly into his eyes. They were piercing her very soul. She couldn't read the emotion in them. Anger? Fear? Something else?

She knew he was waiting for her to say something. What did he want to hear? Was he waiting for her to tell him she *had* been angry? Well, she hadn't. Did he need reassurance that she really did care for them? She had just told him that she did. What was he waiting for?

"If I had grandchildren of my own, I would like them to be just like Kelly and Sean."

He released her hand. "You don't have grandchildren of your own?"

The questioned reminded her that he did not know her. He knew nothing about her. It was as if they had just met. Only they hadn't. As if he could read her thoughts, he reached for his canes and motioned her to follow him as he moved in the direction of the den.

"Let's sit and talk for a while."

"I'll make some decaf coffee then join you."

The Blue Jays baseball game was on the television with the volume turned low. Clarke was sitting on the sofa, his prosthesis removed and his good leg resting on a magazine on the coffee table when she set their cups down.

"I owe you an apology, Maggie."

"For what?"

"It has been all about me these two days I've been home. My needs, my comfort, my grandkids, my daughter, my thoughts, my decisions. All me, me, me. In the meantime, you've been quietly going about seeing to everything without me even asking if you are comfortable or what your thoughts or needs are. I don't even know if you have a family waiting for you to come home. Forgive me. I'm not usually this selfish. I think not anyway." He cast a sideways glance at her as if expecting either an argument or a confirmation from her.

When she didn't respond he reached for his cup and took a sip from it.

"*Do* you have a family waiting for you to return to Ottawa?"

"No, I don't. My husband died three years ago. We had no children, hence no grandchildren. My sister lives in Australia. The only way I know that she's still alive is when I receive her Christmas card each year. My brother Casey lives in Peterborough with his wife and daughter. That's it. No cats. No dogs. I have three close friends who own condos in the same building as mine. You've already met one of them."

"Olivia, of course. Have I not met any of the others?"

"No."

"Why not?"

"I … I don't know." How could she not have trusted her friends' integrity enough to know they would have embraced him if he had two heads and walked on all fours as long as he made her happy?

"I guess we were too busy always and then I came here."

"Ah, yes. The theatre, the dinners out."

Was that scepticism on his face?

"Are they all as amazing as Olivia?"

"Yes, each in her own way." She smiled at the thought of them all attacking Helen's second husband when they thought he was taking advantage of her. They were sure he was up to no good and banded together to protect poor Helen. How wrong they had been. When Helen and Gerald found out, all was forgiven in good time.

"Something is making you smile."

"I was just thinking about an incident involving one of them. It's just a silly memory. When everything settles down and we are eventually back to normal lives in Ottawa, you will meet them."

"Have I been to your place and you to mine?"

"I've been to yours."

The look again. He thinks I've been purposely keeping him from them.

"Have you given any more thought to the future, Clarke?"

"No. I'm so undecided. I really don't know which direction to take. Go? Stay? I think I would be more in control of all the variables in Ottawa. I know the health care system, the services available, which long term facilities are best, how to get around the city. I know who to call. Down here, I feel like a tourist. Like someone waiting to be told what to do, where to go, who to ask. I have to wait for other people to direct me. I prefer operating from my own turf. But I also have to consider the children and Mitchell. He's the biggest unknown. It's not just about me anymore. Nothing is an absolute."

He ran his fingers through his hair. "Maggie, the last thing I remember last night was you saying you would help me carry this burden. Does it make me a selfish bastard if I say I so desperately need you to do just that? Even if I don't know where it's going to take us?"

"I don't care where it takes us, Clarke. I love you and so help me God, I love those children. I would be devastated if you decided I wasn't needed here any longer."

Clarke's arms slid around her waist and his lips met hers.

Chapter Thirty-one

The next two days brought no breaking news. Nothing had changed. The embassy and mission kept in touch but there was nothing new to tell. Kirsten had given signs of coming to but was immediately returned to an induced coma to facilitate healing. She wasn't strong enough for the surgeries yet and until she was, they would keep her sedated.

Olivia left. Margaret drove her into Toronto so she didn't have to carry her own luggage on and off the Go train as she had when she arrived. Somehow, she had managed to fill another suitcase which otherwise might have had to be shipped.

Clarke talked to someone at the local school board to enquire about the possibility of the children being enrolled in the Ottawa Carleton District School system. It was not impossible but involved paperwork.

Mitchell had figuratively disappeared from the face of the earth. There was absolutely no trace of any of the three men. Clarke told Margaret it felt like the police were not putting in a great deal of effort but he didn't want to judge too harshly with nothing on which to base his opinion.

"It looks like the opportunity to go back to Ottawa might be opening. The only major hurdle left is the house. I'll make enquiries about renting it. Sam Burnstrom, next door, is in the real estate business, maybe he can give me some advice."

Margaret was getting concerned by how thin Clarke was. The man hardly rested. If he didn't have his phone in his hand, he was on the computer researching. He was constantly looking for someone somewhere who might help him get his daughter home and find his son-in-law. "Don't forget your follow-up doctor's appointment at the hospital is scheduled for tomorrow." She brushed his shoulder and placed a kiss on the back of his head.

"I don't know why I have to go. There's nothing they can do. My head simply has to heal on its own. There is no dressing to change, no broken bone to X-ray. It's a waste of …" He looked at her. "I'm being difficult aren't I?"

"Yes. I'll feel better after they've tested all your vitals and maybe taken a CT scan. You have lost weight and you're not sleeping well. I hear you moving about the house during the night."

The phone rang before he could argue back. "Yes, Sam. I'm hoping you might give me some advice about renting out Kirsten and Mitch's house for a short term."

Margaret left him to wheel and deal and hopefully get the house issue settled. The cleaning agency was scheduled to come in for several hours today, so she decided to take the kids to an afternoon craft program at the library. She looked at her watch. "Just enough time to fix lunch."

Sean fell with a thud inside the front door he came through it so fast. "Grandpa, Grandpa. Jamie said Daddy was shot dead!" Dirty tears were streaming down his face.

Clarke bumped the doorframe with the wheelchair manoeuvring his way out of the den.

"What are you talking about?"

"He showed me on the news!"

The phone started ringing again. Margaret answered it while Clarke pulled his grandson onto his lap.

It was someone from the Canadian embassy on the phone.

Kelly came into the room. "What did Sean just say? Is it true? Is my dad dead?" She ran to Margaret who was handing the phone to Clarke.

Margaret took both children into the kitchen while Clarke took the call in the den. It was three or four minutes before he came into the kitchen, solemn faced.

"Apparently a man has been found dead in the area but an identity hasn't been made yet. The officials are guessing the victim, who had several gunshot wounds, is either Canadian or American. The local newscaster down there got wind of it and leaked it prematurely. Since embassies from both countries are involved, it appears to now be international news."

He opened his arms to the children and embraced them, both sobbed uncontrollably. The doorbell and the phone both rang at the same time. Clarke still had the phone in his hand so he answered it while Margaret went to the door. It was Sam and Irene Burnstrom on the other side.

They apologized for their son's blurting out the news their family had just seen on the noon broadcast from one of the news channels. They told Clarke to do whatever he had to do and they would take care of the Sennetts' home in one way or another.

Clarke and Margaret had barely said goodbye to their neighbours when the house cleaners arrived.

"Oh dear. This is not a good time. An emergency has just come up. You can bill us for today, but I'll call the office and reschedule for another day."

The children were standing on either side of Clarke as he talked to someone from the Mission.

It wasn't until late evening they received word that the body had been identified as the American passenger travelling on the same bus. The police were still searching but there were no signs of the other two men. The Hamilton area local television station had phoned and knocked on the door looking for an interview now that it was common knowledge Mitchell was missing in the jungle and his wife detained in hospital down there because of life-threatening injuries. Clarke phoned the hospital in Lima and insisted his daughter be kept from hearing of these events at all costs.

Margaret lay with the children until they had fallen asleep on the pull-out bed in the den. The young people needed the company of the adults and each other. She watched as Clarke took care of each detail looking more and more haggard with each phone call. She wanted to unplug every phone in the house and remove the battery from his cell phone but of course that was impossible. Phones were the only link, the only means of communication between him and his daughter. He seemed to age with every passing hour. When he started rubbing his leg where his prosthetic usually was attached, she knew he could not keep this up indefinitely. He would end up in the hospital again.

"Let me take the phone calls for an hour or so while you close your eyes. I promise to wake you if it's someone with actual news rather than just looking for it."

"I don't know if I could sleep, Maggie. There is so much running through my head. My baby girl could die any minute and she's all alone. There's no one to hug her or whisper to her that she's loved."

"I'm surprised that you, a man of such faith, doesn't realize that the one who loves her even more than you has her wrapped in His healing arms and is whispering words of love, hope and strength in her ear. She knows she's loved and that even if the worst happens, she is not alone."

Clarke raised his tired head and looked at Margaret. "You are so right. I should be ashamed of myself for wallowing in pity and fear. Sit and pray with me."

Chapter Thirty-two

On the premise that no news is good news, they get through the next two days. Then Sam Burnstrom rang the doorbell after supper on the second day.

"If you are still interested in putting this house up for rent, Irene and I are interested in signing a lease for it."

He went on to explain that they had been trying to talk Irene's aging parents in to moving to Hamilton from their rural home near Tillsonburg for quite a while. The older folks lived in the old farmhouse they had bought fifty years before when they were first married and were reluctant to leave it. Sam and Irene had spent two days talking to them and had finally persuaded them to try city living for six to twelve months and this house with its ramps and accessibility was perfect for them.

They agreed on a monthly rental rate and also settled on a written agreement rather than a lease in case Kirsten improved or Mitch returned and needed it back before a year passed. It was to be rented furnished, with personal items removed and stored, until such time as they were needed.

With that off his plate, Clarke showed visible signs of relief and Margaret now knew the die was cast and they would all be on their way to Ottawa within a couple of weeks. The children had agreed to the move. The need of attending a different school had taken on the mood of a new adventure.

They were happy that Margaret was going to be a major part of their lives — the next best thing to their mother being home.

Their grandpa and grandma, as Clarke had given permission for Margaret to be called, were going to be caring for them until their parents were able to do so again.

"Margaret, are you up to this?" Helen sounded worried.

"To be honest, I'm frightened right out of my boots. Being a full-time grandmother is exhausting but when I tuck them in at night and hear that word it is all so worth it."

"And Clarke? Is he worth it also?"

"I love that man so much if he asked me to take in a boarding house full of his grandchildren, I would."

"Olivia seems quite smitten with him. Everything out of her mouth is Clarke this and Clarke that. He has divine eyes, a sexy mouth, he's so attentive and thoughtful."

"Ha, ha. He was taken with her as well. He asked if the rest of you were as marvellous as she. I'd better watch myself. He's liable to be stolen right out from under me."

"So you are coming home with the children to get them settled in school? They'll stay with you for a week or so before Clarke comes?"

"Yes, we have a busy week ahead of us packing up all the personal items and putting them in storage. We thought of hiring the storage company to do it for us, but it would be as much work to sort through everything and separate it from what is staying as it would be to do it ourselves. We want to keep the children's things separate in case we need anything over the winter. I'm just getting worried about Clarke. He's physically not as strong as he lets on he is."

"I'm worried about you, Margaret. You are probably doing more than you should be as well. Don't forget you're on the downhill side of sixty. You're not forty anymore. What is there to do after you and the children leave?"

"I'm as healthy as I've ever been. We'll get it all packed and stored, hopefully. By then the children will have to leave for school but Clarke will stay behind to make sure a few repairs are done and to have the house cleaned after all the boxes are gone and the closets and drawers are emptied. He has to speak to his daughter's lawyer, too, about all the legalities involved with the rental, the liability for the house, and also there is so much paperwork needed for Kirsten's medical care and transport home."

"I'm exhausted just listening to you. Will you be flying?"

"No. We'll take the train. There is a fair amount of stuff to bring and the neighbours have offered to drive us in to Union Station in Toronto so that the luggage just has to be handled once. We may ship some of the boxes just before we leave. Helen, I'll so look forward to an afternoon of cards once we're all settled. I'll talk to you soon."

Early the following afternoon, the doorbell rang and Margaret heard the door open and a male voice call out her name.

"Gerald? Gerald is that you?" She couldn't believe her ears.

When she reached the door Helen and Gerald were standing in the entryway.

"What are you doing here?"

"Mercier packing, moving, storage and delivery at your service, Madam."

"What?" Margaret brought her hands to her cheeks

The sound of Clarke's canes was preceding him down the hallway. He looked askance at the couple standing in the foyer.

"Clarke, this is Helen and Gerald Mercier, my friends from Ottawa."

"Don't worry we're not looking for a place to stay." Gerald extended his hand as he spoke.

Helen stepped forward and patted Clarke's arm. "We've already checked in to a hotel and we're here to help."

"Help?" Clarke appeared at a loss for words.

"We heard you were in need of packers, cleaners, babysitters, delivery guys, whatever. We figured we fit in to at least one of those niches." Gerald was still shaking Clarke's hand. "You give us a job, point us in the right direction and we'll do our best."

Clarke looked from Gerald to Helen to Margaret.

"I told you I had the best friends in the world."

"Whose big blue van is that in our driveway?" Sean came running up the front steps.

After coffee and sandwiches, everyone had a job to do. Margaret was to help Sean clean out his closet and drawers and set up different piles — things to take, things to pack, and things to give away. Helen would help Kelly do the same thing and the men were going to tackle the garage.

Gerald and Clarke went to a local storage facility and came home with boxes, packing paper and tape which were divided among the three sets of workers. Clarke also paid rent for a small storage unit for six months so that once things were packed they could be immediately taken out from underfoot to the facility. By suppertime, they had two bedrooms and the garage stripped. Kelly said she would sleep with Margaret and Sean insisted on spreading out his sleeping bag in his grandpa's bedroom. They washed the bedding, folded it and placed it all at the foot of each bed.

Clarke looked around and commented that everyone, even the children, looked exhausted. He insisted they have pizza delivered. No one argued with him.

Kelly and Sean were dead to the world by nine o'clock. Gerald and Helen were enjoying the fresh evening air by the pool. The late-August evenings were noticeably cooler. Clarke moved his wheelchair through the patio doors followed by Margaret who was carrying a tray with cocktails and a plate of veggies and cheese on it.

"I think you helped us knock a couple of days off our

schedule. At this rate, I may be able to leave with Margaret and the children."

Gerald finished munching on a carrot stick before saying, "Helen and I were hoping you, Margaret and the children could accompany us back."

Clarke started to reply when Gerald interrupted. "Hear me out. If you don't mind riding in a cargo van, there's no reason why we can't rent one, load it with all the boxes going to Ottawa and you and I can ride together while the women take the kids in our van. It saves train costs, shipping costs, and we can take everything from the fridge, freezer and pantry you might otherwise toss or leave. Helen figures between her and Margaret they can clean this house as well as, or maybe even better than the professionals."

Clarke was stumped for words. "You would do all that for someone you don't even know?"

Helen piped up. "We know Margaret and if she's taken a shine to you and your grandchildren, that's good enough for us."

"You are wasting your breath if you think you might win this one, Clarke." Gerald took Helen's hand in his. "It took a while before it permeated this thick skull of mine, but I eventually caught on that these four women are joined at the hip. You take one, you take them all."

Helen poked him in the ribs and made him laugh. "But quite frankly I wouldn't have it any other way. They're like a family and when a family member needs help, everyone pitches in and gets the job done. After speaking with Margaret last night, Helen called the girls together and we sat down and figured out a plan. That's why we're here."

"Clarke, there's no way we could sit idly at home twiddling our thumbs knowing you and Margaret had so much work to do. We just couldn't let you call in outside help and travel at two different times and separate yourself from the children when we can get it done in time for you to all travel together." The earnest look on Helen's face told Margaret that no one would have kept her and Gerald at home when help was needed.

Clarke shook his head. "I don't know how to thank you. It bothered me that I had to send Maggie ahead with the children. I know they didn't mind and Maggie probably didn't either, but I did. This isn't what she bought into." He spread his arms to include the whole house. "I … I don't know how I'd have gotten this far without her."

"Helen and I have been through a couple of hard times and Margaret and the other women were right there to offer help. If it's going to take a village to get through all this, then we have one at 73 Windsor Street. So accept it, Clarke, and let us help."

"I'm not going to refuse. I recognize friendship when it's being offered and I've never been one to turn away from a friend."

Margaret offered to refill everyone's glasses and took the tray inside. Gerald and Clarke started discussing what size vehicle they might need. Helen followed her friend into the kitchen.

"Margaret, are you packing Kirsten's good china and crystal for storage?"

"No, Clarke and I discussed it but I think it should be safe with adults living here. It has survived Kelly and Sean so far and I believe any family entertaining will be done next door."

Helen looked through to the dining room and remarked, "It's a beautiful pattern, very elegant."

"I understand it was Kirsten's mother's. When Clarke moved into the condo after Kirsten was married he gave it to her, along with the crystal and silverware."

"How old was Kirsten when her mother died?"

"I'm not sure of her age exactly but she was just a small child. Clarke raised her on his own."

"Is she a minister also?"

"No, but she is quite involved in the church apparently as is her husband."

"Clarke never remarried?"

"No."

Chapter Thirty-three

Three full days of purging, packing, and cleaning brought them to a point where the actual move was imminent. It was decided that the women and children would stay the final night in the hotel where Helen and Gerald had been staying. The men would stay in the house. Clarke had insisted he wanted to stay "just in case". When Margaret had expressed concern about him staying alone as he was on the brink of exhaustion, Gerald offered to remain with him. Phone calls to the landline were being forwarded to Clarke's cell phone. A cargo van had been reserved for the following day and all the paperwork for the house rental was complete. They only needed to give their neighbours the keys.

Margaret wasn't fooled. She knew Clarke felt his daughter's presence in the house and was reluctant to leave. If she were in his shoes, she would have foolishly wanted her daughter and son-in-law to walk through the front door and realize this had all been a bad dream. He was breaking a connection. Poor man. How helpless he must feel.

Kelly and Sean spent the afternoon with friends before leaving to make new ones in Ottawa. They weren't the first children to leave best friends, school and bedrooms behind, especially bedrooms that had been decorated to match their own personalities and dreams. The difference here was that they were moving without the comfort and excitement of having their parents accompany them to a new location, a new home where they could live out their dreams and fantasies.

Again, she thanked God for her friends. They were not only a huge help but also a huge distraction. Gerald had shown Sean how, then allowed him, to handle a screwdriver all the while talking soccer and baseball. Kelly had been busy filling Helen in on all the plans she had for university and life after school. Helen encouraged her dreams and offered suggestions. She taught her how to fold fitted sheets properly so they didn't look like lumps with socks or underwear caught in the elasticized corners.

Clarke had been relieved he didn't have to deal with draining the pool. The Burnstroms didn't have one in their yard so had asked that it be left as is so they and their son could enjoy it. By the time evening arrived, the rooms in the house were devoid of all personal articles. Closets and drawers were empty, vacuumed and scrubbed. Oven cleaned and refrigerator interior gleaming. All the bathrooms but one had been scoured. Laundry room was tidy and clean. There was even room inside the garage to actually park a car.

The plans were for everyone to arrive at the house by eight in the morning, coffee and muffins in hand. Gerald was to have the moving van ready to load the boxes, toys, bicycles and clothing. Suitcases with immediate needs would go in the back of Gerald's van, along with the vacuum cleaner and the last of the rags and brooms. If all went well, they would be on the road by ten o'clock and in Ottawa well before suppertime.

Helen and Gerald had been staying in a mini-suite in a nearby hotel. It had two beds and hide-a-bed sofa. Since Gerald was staying at the house with Clarke, Margaret and the children would join Helen in their suite. Kelly would sleep with Margaret and Sean on the sofa bed. Before leaving the house that evening, Margaret caught Clarke alone in the garage where he was leaning the bicycles against a stack of packed boxes.

"Promise me you won't stay up too late trying to finish

everything by yourself." She ran her hand down his cheek and onto his shoulder. "You look so tired and tomorrow will be another long stressful day."

He took her hand and kissed her palm. Tears brimmed in his eyes. He pulled her to him and kissed her gently. "I … I …" Words failed him.

Margaret laid her head against his chest and whispered. "I know. I know."

"I promise you when we are in Ottawa and things all get sorted, I will try my best to show you what you mean to me." He kissed her again before they walked into the kitchen.

The children fell asleep faster than Margaret had thought they would. She and Helen sat at the little round table typical of most hotel rooms and enjoyed a cold iced tea from the bar fridge.

"I guess by the time we hit the road in the morning we'll have missed most of the heavy traffic. I haven't travelled the 401 since I used to come down with Edward on some of his business trips. I hated the highway congestion with a passion. With Gerald we seem to fly to Toronto more often than drive. Although you still have to go through traffic to and from the various airports. Does Clarke drive?"

"Oh yes. He met me at the airport when I came down. His right leg is fine. It's his left leg that is missing."

"I haven't wanted to pry, Margaret, but how did he lose his leg?"

"It was a childhood accident. He's able to take his disability for granted now but from what he told me, his school years are not fond memories. He was bullied a bit and left out of a lot of activities. He said he learned at an early age that adults were more understanding of his incapacity for active play, so consequently he tended to spend more time with them playing chess and darts, and, of course, reading was where he could live vicariously through others' lives."

She took a deep breath. "He doesn't like to talk about it, but his accident is a lifelong reminder of the one and only time he really lost control. The taunts of the bullies in the neighbourhood about his slight build and lack of physical prowess finally got under his skin enough to make him disobey his father. Apparently, there was an abandoned building a few blocks from his home. On the way to and from school in the winter time, some of the more daring kids would climb up onto the roof and use the long slope as a toboggan run into a snowbank on the ground. There were a couple of old rusting vehicles in a space between the roof and the landing spot so the takeoff from the edge of the roof had to be just right. Clarke was taunted regularly because he wouldn't make the jump — a rite of passage so to speak. He knew he wasn't strong enough to gain the speed and momentum required to make the ride safely, plus his father had loudly proclaimed that his son was never to participate in such a dangerous, foolhardy stunt just to prove himself to a bunch of louts. One day, the boys had been particularly hard on him, driving him to tears, calling him a sissy and a coward in front of a number of his friends so he took the dare. He didn't clear the vehicles and the result was he mangled his left leg enough it had to be amputated, and a couple of breaks in his right leg healed badly so that he has a weakness in it as well. His father never totally forgave him for his disobedience, but Clarke feels it was his father's disappointment in his son's weakness of character that bothered the man more. He resolved never to lose his temper or control again and he has an abiding love for the underdog."

Helen placed a hand on Margaret's arm. "What a testament to Clarke's character. He certainly doesn't appear to suffer any lack of confidence and seems to live life with zest."

"That he does. He taught me a great lesson about enjoying

life fully."

"When did he become a minister?"

"It was during his time in university that he first felt the call, but it wasn't until he met his wife that he answered it."

Sean stirred and started to whimper.

"I think it's time for us to turn out the lights and hit the sack ourselves."

By 9:45 the following morning, they were crossing the Burlington Skyway, the bridge that joins Hamilton on the south side of Lake Ontario to Burlington on the north side.

Sean was excited and talking non-stop about the things he was going to do in Ottawa. They had visited their grandfather several times and had seen most of the tourist attractions. Now he was looking forward to checking other places and events off his list. He was looking forward to fall and going up to the Champlain Lookout in the Gatineau Hills where he had read you can see the whole Ottawa Valley. The next thing was to go river rafting on the Ottawa River. His parents had kept telling him he was too young, but he hoped his grandpa would take him. His list went on and on. Margaret smiled thinking he had forgotten that this wasn't a vacation and he'd be in school full time.

Kelly was quiet, gloomily watching the miles slide by her window. She was the deeper thinker of the two and Margaret wondered what thoughts were going through her mind as they drove farther and farther away from her childhood home, the home to which she had hoped her parents would soon return. She seemed more sullen than sad. Could she be feeling a little anger at being uprooted and taken away?

At the truck stop where they stopped for lunch she quickly ran to her grandfather's side and inquired about his well-being. "Are you tired, Grandpa? We are over halfway there, Helen said."

"I'm fine, honey. This is the longest I've been able to sit and relax since we learned of your parents' accident." He ruffled her hair affectionately. "How about you?"

"I'm okay. I've been worried that this long drive would tire you out. I don't want your brain getting sick again." She hugged his waist and asked if she could sit beside him in the restaurant.

"Of course, you can." He recognized the difference in her mood. He caught Margaret looking their way and winked.

It was not yet four o'clock when the two vehicles drove up to the front of Clarke's condominium. He lived about five blocks west and south of Margaret's place. Sean had fallen asleep and had to be awakened. One elevator had been reserved to facilitate the move of boxes into Clarke's condo and down to the storage room adjacent to the underground car park.

By six o'clock both vehicles had been emptied. The Merciers said their good-byes brushing off Clarke's and Margaret's attempts at saying thank you. Helen was to follow Gerald to the U-Haul drop-off location; then they were going home. Margaret said she would take a taxi home later after the children were settled in.

It had already been agreed upon that Kelly would take the guest bedroom and Sean would make the sofa bed in the den his sleeping place temporarily. In the coming days, they would purchase a bed for the boy and turn the den into a proper bedroom. Clarke's bedroom was large enough to hold his desk and bookshelves. Only the sofa would have to find a new home. All of this would wait until he had recuperated from the hectic previous two weeks.

Margaret had found chicken nuggets and french fries in the freezer which she placed in the oven. Some frozen mixed veggies rounded out the meal. Kelly still appeared to be in a funk but Sean was adapting well.

While the children were unpacking and finding drawer and

closet space for the things in the suitcases, Margaret took advantage of the break to talk to Clarke.

"I think it might be best if I left shortly so that you and the children have time to unwind before all of you go to bed. You've hardly had a minute alone with them since their parents' accident and I sense that Kelly needs some reassurance from you. She was quiet all the way here and she seemed to want you close to her during our lunch break."

"You are so astute, Margaret. I had really wanted some time with you this evening but you're right. I've got to quit thinking about what I want. She did seem a little clingy at the restaurant."

"You are the one constant in all of this, Clarke. With the future of her parents up in the air, you are the only one she knows for sure is going to be here for them. I think she has to know that you are strong and healthy — that you'll be here to take care of them no matter what. This will be her first time going to school on that first day without a parent to take her. She'll have no friends to meet up with and share stories about their summer holidays."

"Will I see you tomorrow?"

"Probably. I don't know what's waiting for me at home. The girls have been collecting my mail and checking my place, but I'll have to go through everything. I'll call you later on tomorrow morning. I will say good night to the children while you arrange for a taxi or uber for me." She hugged each child and promised to talk to them the following day.

"Don't forget you promised to take me to your hairdresser so I can get my hair cut before school." Kelly held the hug longer than usual.

"I'll call her first thing in the morning. You have my e-mail address, so you can send me a note to remind me when you wake up."

Sean also squeezed her tight. "Thank you for being our

grandma. I hope you'll still let us call you that now that we're in Ottawa."

"Of course, darling. I won't stop being your grandmother."

An hour later Margaret flopped into her favourite chair in her own condo and started to cry.

Chapter Thirty-four

She was physically and emotionally drained. It had been less than a month before that she had left this very room full of joy and dreams. Joy at having been invited to spend the next couple of weeks with a man she was deeply fond of. Had she been in love with him at that point? Or had it just been feelings of friendship with anticipation of more? Her dreams had included spending the rest of her life with a man just like Clarke. Not a dashing, handsome, virile man but a man with deeper qualities, a man capable of compassion, caring and, she was sure, deep and everlasting love. They had shared many wonderful days and evenings together before he left to take care of his grandchildren. Would they have days and evenings like that again?

The ringing of the phone broke her reverie.

"Hello."

"I'll bet you are exhausted so I won't keep you. I just wanted to make sure you were home safe and sound." Olivia, the eldest of her friends, was always the mother hen. Even when spending her winters in Florida, she had to rule the roost. Weekly phone calls home to ensure everyone was surviving without her were the norm.

"Yes, I am tired. I'm going to sit in a nice relaxing bath then go to bed. Tomorrow is another day. I'm not sure who dropped off the fresh cream and fruit, but it is most welcome. I'll give Sarah a call when we hang up."

"Okay, kiddo. We'll talk in the morning. It's nice to have you back home again."

Margaret made the phone call to Sarah, the only one who had not yet met Clarke. Sarah had been married three times and didn't have much faith in long-term relationships. She dated occasionally but if a man showed any signs of wanting something more permanent, he was politely sent on his way. After saying good night to Sarah, she poured her bath.

The condo had always been her haven. For the past three years she had found comfort in the quiet and solitude of these five rooms. The contemporary style furniture with smooth clean lines matched her lifestyle. There hadn't been children, the factor that usually facilitated a need for sturdy design with fabric and colouring to withstand spills and indoor play. She and Hugh had opted for lighter colours and clean smooth design, even her bedroom suite had more of a plain Quaker look to it.

Margaret looked around her. Something was missing. It lacked the warmth, the comfort that it usually held. Her glance took in the gleam of the hardwood floors, the polished furniture, the toss cushions neatly placed at each end of the sofa. Nothing seemed out of place. *Oh well, I'll figure it out in the morning.*

Morning arrived with the ringing of the phone. She glanced about and saw that light was peaking along the edges of her blinds. It had been her first sound sleep in three weeks.

She picked up the phone and before she had it to her ear, she heard, "Grandma, I hope I didn't wake you up. Grandpa made me wait until eight o'clock before I could call you."

Margaret sighed. This is what was missing in her condo. The sound of children.

"Good morning, Kelly. Did you have a good sleep?"

"Yes, I did. Did you?"

Margaret could hear Sean's voice in the background. "Sean, I'm talking to her right now. Wait till I'm finished. Sorry, Grandma, Sean is acting like a spoiled brat."

She could hear more noise in the background then Kelly spoke again.

"We were wondering if you will come to have lunch with us."

"Oh my. I haven't even thought about breakfast yet."

"Grandpa made us his world-famous pancakes."

"Then maybe he won't feel like cooking for a guest at lunch time."

"He said we could ask you." Margaret could hear a slight shuffling sound, then a whispered, "I think he's hoping you'll come."

A smile shaped her lips. "Then I will be there. I need a little time to take care of some things here, but I'll try to be there for around noon or so."

She dressed quickly and made a cup of coffee with her Keurig. After a phone call to Sarah with an invitation to join her for coffee, she set about opening her mail which had been collected and stacked on the dining room table. Most of her bills were paid by automatic withdrawal from her bank account so sorting the envelopes was not a daunting task. A letter from her niece, Chelsea, and another from a nephew of Hugh's inviting her to his university graduation were the only two pieces of mail of any real interest.

Sarah arrived and after hugs were exchanged the two women spent an hour catching up on the past four weeks.

"So you don't even get a day off before you have to go running over and give the children more of your time?"

Margaret was taken back by Sarah's blunt assessment of the situation.

"I don't *have* to go running anywhere. I *want* to go over and join them for lunch."

"From what I hear, Clarke is a real gem so I would have thought he would at least allow you a day to rest and recuperate before allowing the children to bother you."

"Sarah, listen to you. The children aren't bothering me. I hated leaving all of them in a state of displaced emotions last night. If there had been room for me I would have gladly stayed with them."

"Of course. I was being thoughtless. And I guess being a man of the cloth, it's inappropriate for you to share his bed with the children there."

"Share his … No. No. You have this all wrong. Clarke and I are not sleeping together."

"But you said he had taken care of all your ailments before he left for Hamilton. You gave us the impression, well, the impression that you were. You never gave us reason to believe otherwise."

Margaret fixed Sarah another cup of coffee.

"I do not suffer any ailments because he makes me so profoundly happy, not because we are having sex. He has given me a new lease on life, a reason to quit dwelling on aches and pains, real or imagined. Oh, Sarah, I can hardly wait for you to meet him so you can see the reason I want to spend every waking moment of the day with him."

"So Clarke really is Superman."

Margaret hesitated then laughed. "Now I get it. Clarke — Superman. I can be so slow sometimes."

She turned in her chair so that she was facing her friend. "To be honest with you, I don't know if Clarke and I will ever have sex and I don't care."

"Wow. He must be some man. No sex. A physical handicap. And baggage in the form of two grandchildren." She took Margaret's hand and continued before Margaret could speak. "Forgive me. I was feeling a little anger about a situation I guess he has no control over. I'll have to meet the man and I'm sure I'll fall in love with him just as Olivia and Helen have. The kids I'm not sure about. I still think that after all you've done for them, they could have waited at least a day before dragging you back into the whirlwind their lives have become."

"This doesn't sound like you, Sarah. You're usually more understanding."

"I'm just hoping you haven't fallen into a pit that might prove too much for you over the long haul. What if his daughter never gets better? What if the son-in-law is never found? Are you prepared to spend every single day for the rest of your life caring for two young children — driving them to dancing lessons, soccer, hockey or whatever interests them? Let alone homework, school friends and their social lives. You have always been a little fragile, Margaret. Hugh always looked after you, even spoiled you a little. I would guess in your current situation it's you who is the caregiver and nurturer. Are you up to that?"

Margaret wanted this conversation to be over. Her friend did not understand what it was like to finally be needed. Maybe this was the reason for Sarah's numerous marriages. Maybe she wasn't willing to give more than she received. She wanted Sarah to meet Clarke and the children and get to know them before making these wild assumptions.

"I'm up to anything this loving family asks of me."

Sarah stood and when Margaret did also, Sarah pulled her into a warm embrace then brushed her cheek with a kiss. "What makes you happy makes me happy. Bring Superman and your grandchildren to dinner at my place tomorrow."

With that she was out the door.

Chapter Thirty-five

Margaret called her hair stylist for two appointments for the following day, got her car out of the underground parking then left to keep her lunch date.

When she arrived at Clarke's, the living and dining rooms were crowded with half-empty boxes. Sean was upset because Kelly had her clothes almost all put away, but he had no dresser in which to put his. Clarke had emptied a couple in the bureau in his room, but Sean was wishing for one in his own room.

"We may have to go furniture shopping sooner than I had anticipated."

"I noticed a television commercial on the TV last night promoting a big sale at The Brick. I'll bet they'll deliver for a small fee."

"Can we go there, Grandpa?"

"I suppose. We may as well pick out a matching bed while we're at it."

"Can we get Spiderman sheets for it too?"

Clarke rolled his eyes and agreed. "In the meantime, you put some of these things in my room so we can get rid of a few boxes. I don't think they'll deliver today. Where are we going to eat our meals?"

"Kelly, will you help me?"

The two busied themselves sorting out which clothes to put where. While they were distracted, Clarke asked Margaret to join him on the balcony.

"I received a call from the hospital in Lima this morning. Kirsten was to undergo surgery today but they have to delay it for a few more days because of infection."

"Oh no. Does this create any major problems?"

"I don't know. They'll call again this evening if anything changes or her condition worsens. I'm so worried that with each passing day she's not receiving any of the surgeries she needs."

"Clarke, I pray so hard that one of these days the news coming out of there will be news of healing and hope." She looked at his eyes and face. "How are you today? Did you sleep well now that you're back in your own bed?"

"Yes, I slept fairly soundly. I'm waiting on a call from the school board to confirm which school the kids will be enrolled in. Once we know that, and if they'll be bused, that will be one more item off my to-do list."

"Did you call your doctor?"

"I see him on Thursday."

"We have an invitation to Sarah Eisenboch's for dinner tomorrow evening. All of us, children included. She wants to meet Superman."

"Superman?"

"I'm afraid that's an endearing handle you may be stuck with."

He looked surprised. "I've been called a lot of things in my life, but Superman? Really?"

"It should be Superhuman for all you're contending with right now."

"I'm only doing what I can. I wish it was more. My daughter needs me. I think a familiar voice, a squeeze of her hand, a kiss on the cheek all might go a long way to help ease her suffering. She'd at least know her daddy was there."

Margaret slid her arm around his waist. "If I could help you get there I would, but I don't think you are anywhere near strong enough to travel that far."

"I know. It's just the ramblings of a wistful old man."

"Clarke, you are still a young man. You know I'm talking about your own near fatal accident and hospital stay."

His eyes lingered on hers. "I wish I could say I remember all our time together, Maggie. I want so badly to get back what you say we had before. I know you. I anticipate your words, knowing exactly what they'll be. I know all the nuances. I know what is you and what isn't you. I just can't remember the times we shared." He brushed his lips across her forehead.

They ate lunch then Margaret drove them to a Brick store in Nepean. Before long, they had picked out a single bed and matching chest of drawers. Arrangements for delivery were made for two days later. One more stop completed their shopping with a bed-in-a-bag ensemble of Spiderman sheets, pillowcase and quilt.

They decided to make a stop at Dow's Lake to let the children walk around and get some fresh air and exercise.

While Margaret and Clarke were sitting on a bench watching the children run about on the lawn, he took her hand. "The children seem to be adjusting well."

"The poor darlings. It's a good thing they have each other."

"Yes. Like any brother and sister they fight like little devils sometimes but they really do support each other. Kirsten and Mitch have done an excellent job in raising them. I only hope someday they'll all be back living under their familiar roof once again."

His hand tightened on Margaret's. "If it weren't for you, I'd still be running in circles in Hamilton trying to figure out what to with them."

"You would have figured out a plan of your own and implemented it in your own intelligent way."

"I know I certainly wouldn't be sitting here in this beautiful spot watching them play like they didn't have a care in the world. Thank you, Maggie, for getting us to where we are now. Tremendous thanks to your great circle of friends also. To think they just dropped everything, put their lives on hold and made the trip down to help us. I'm still flabbergasted."

"I was surprised too. I know how good they are, but I'm overwhelmed by all they did also."

The children had moved beyond their line of vision so Margaret stood and looked around then saw them over near the water watching a large pleasure boat coming in to dock. She motioned them away from the water and watched as Sean tugged at Kelly's hair and ran across the open space. She took off after him and they ended up playing a form of tag.

Clarke watched as Margaret walked back toward him with the lowering sun behind her. When she neared he held up his phone and snapped a picture. She laughed as she sat. "I can't look very picture worthy with my hair blowing all over the place."

He pulled the picture up on the screen of his phone. The light from the sun had formed a kind of halo or aura around her body. It startled her as it made her look like a saintly figure surrounded by light.

"Good. I was hoping the camera would capture it. I knew I could never describe how you looked as you were walking toward me."

She continued to stare at the photo. It was almost eerie in a serene kind of way.

"My angel."

"Pardon?"

"You're the angel God has given me to watch over me."

"I'm not quite an angel, Clarke. You haven't seen my temper." She tried to smile.

"Really? Never? I feel cheated because I want to remember meeting you that first time. I want to remember our conversations, our times together. I want to remember falling in love with you because I know I must have. Maggie, have patience with me. I don't think I could go on without you."

"Grandpa, we're hungry. Is it time for supper yet?"

Chapter Thirty-six

It was late in the afternoon the next day when Clarke and Sean arrived at Margaret's apartment. She and Kelly had gone for their haircuts during the afternoon and Kelly had come home with her afterward. Clarke was walking quite steadily using his canes. His strength was slowly returning, and Margaret hoped the return of the memory gap would soon follow. They were expected at Sarah's around six o'clock for supper.

They were barely inside Margaret's door when Sean blurted out, "The hospital phoned Grandpa and my mom is having an operation tomorrow morning."

Margaret looked at Clarke. "Yes. They called just as we were getting dressed to come here."

"Her infection is gone?"

"I didn't actually talk to the doctor. It was someone relaying a message from the doctor. Maybe we'll get a chance to talk later."

She understood. He didn't want to discuss it in front of the children.

Sarah was somewhat of a gourmet cook with menus suiting an adult palate rather than the tender taste buds of children. Margaret was worried that the children might not find her cooking to their liking. She need not have worried. The chicken was cooked without any rich sauces, but Margaret knew the breaded coating was made from something healthy and exotic.

The baby roasted potatoes again had just enough flavour to distinguish them from the run-of-the-mill servings you would receive in family restaurants. The vegetables were done with a honey coating which the children found quite enjoyable. Dessert consisted of the old standard: brownies and vanilla ice cream.

The meal, the congeniality of the guests, the impeccable manners of the youngsters and the warmth of the hostess all contributed to an enjoyable evening. Margaret let her breath out at the end of it. Sarah didn't question Clarke endlessly about his life and his intentions. The children didn't spill anything on the rug. Margaret sensed that Clarke had connected with Sarah and all was good.

When Margaret carried some of the dishes into the kitchen after the meal was over, Sarah whispered in her ear, "He's a keeper." No sooner did she have the words out than Kelly and Sean came through the door carrying their own emptied plates.

They went back to Margaret's condo after dinner and the children became absorbed in a coffee table book she had taken out for them to look at. It had a collection of National Geographic pictures of jungles and jungle animals of the world.

She brought Clarke a cup of tea which she knew he enjoyed in the evening. This was the last week the kids would be allowed to stay up a little later on weekday evenings. School would be starting, and they'd need their sleep.

"Do you know what time Kirsten's surgery is tomorrow?"

"No. I will call again after the kids are in bed and see if I can get more information. This is the worst part of being thousands of miles away from her. Even if Mitch was with her, it would be a lot easier. I just keep thinking about her being there all alone."

"Will you call me when you know something?"

"Of course." He smiled at Margaret. "Your hair looks lovely."

He took her hand in his. "Oh, the nails are beautiful too."

"Kelly, did you enjoy going to the salon today?"

The girl was so enthralled with the pictures it took her a moment to respond. "Yes, Grandpa, I even got a manicure. Look." She held her softly coloured nails out for him to see.

"Well, aren't you special. They look lovely, honey. Did you notice your brother also got a haircut?"

"Yeah, I already told him it was cool even though he didn't say anything about my hair."

Sean had tuned them out. "Kelly, look at these baby leopards. They're so small they look like kittens."

Margaret turned to Clarke again. "You're walking much better today. You must be feeling stronger."

"I am. I'm feeling more like my old self."

She sensed he had something on his mind and didn't reply. When he didn't add anything she just smiled and let it go.

After they had gone, she gave Olivia her nightly call and told her how much they had enjoyed dinner at Sarah's. "Clarke said Kirsten is having surgery tomorrow."

"What kind of surgery?"

"I don't know. He's going to call the hospital after Kelly and Sean are in bed and see if he can talk to a doctor, even if it's not the surgeon. It's killing him being here knowing she's all alone down there."

"I guess it's impossible for him to go now that he has the responsibility of the children."

"I would look after the children for a week or so if he could go down there but he's not up to travelling that far yet. At least not by himself."

"Don't they start school next week?"

"Yes, that's why it would be easier. They would be gone all day."

"You're sure a glutton for punishment, Margaret. Aren't you exhausted from all the turmoil of the past three or four weeks?"

"I'm feeling a little weary, yes, but I can't imagine what it must be like for Clarke being stuck here and his daughter needing him there. You know, the kids are good and once they're in school they're only around for a few hours in the evening. At least he can keep in touch with the hospital and get updates. It's not like it was when they were missing." She bid Olivia good night and promised to call in the morning.

Margaret was lying in bed watching the late news when the phone rang.

"Hi, beautiful."

"Clarke." She couldn't help smiling at his softly spoken words.

"I like your friend, Sarah. She's quite a cook."

"Yes, she gives some mean dinner parties. You should taste her Chinese cooking."

"Kelly commented that her china wasn't quite as nice as yours. It's funny the things kids notice."

"They were so good this evening. Their table manners were impeccable."

"Yes, I'm pretty proud of them. That outfit you had on tonight, do you have earrings the same colour?"

She hesitated. "Yes, I do."

"Hmm. It seemed to me that something was missing. They were little crystal drops."

"Clarke, I …" She was breathless with excitement.

"Sweetheart, it's coming but it's slow. I'll get there. I know I will. Patience."

"I know you will, too. I have faith. Have you called the hospital yet?"

"I'll do that when we hang up. I just needed to hear your voice once more before I call there."

"I'm sure you must be on pins and needles wondering and worrying about her surgery. Will you call me again after you've spoken with them?"

"Sometimes it takes a while before I can get through to someone who can give me answers. Will you still be awake?"

"I'll be waiting. It doesn't matter what time it is."

An hour and a half later the phone rang. She was in the living room reading a mystery novel but finding it hard to concentrate. Poor Clarke. What horrible agony he must be going through with his only child on another continent, not knowing if she was going to survive impending surgery and unable to go to her.

"Hi, darling." She tried to keep the fear from her voice.

"Hi, Maggie." He took a deep breath. "It took three phone calls before I finally was able to speak to someone other than a nurse who has no authority to give out information. It's so frustrating. Then the added language problem."

"So you were able to learn something then?"

"Yes." She could hear a quiver in his voice. "They are operating on her spine. They have to remove a chip that is causing pain and interfering with a nerve."

"That sounds serious."

"It is. The possibility is there that the surgery could leave her paralyzed."

"Oh, Clarke. Oh, no. Is it absolutely necessary for them to do this?"

"Apparently, the pain she's suffering is excruciating. That's why they've been keeping her in a coma. They have no alternative but to go forward with it."

"What time is it scheduled for?"

"First thing in the morning — seven o'clock. That's eight our time."

"Please call me when you hear anything."

"I will, sweetheart. Good night."

"Good night."

She held the phone against her chest. How she wished he had

said he loved her.

Stop being so selfish, Margaret. His mind is on his daughter's suffering.

Chapter Thirty-seven

At eight forty-five the next morning, her door buzzer sounded.

"Hello?"

"Grandma, we came for pancakes. Can we come in?"

When she opened her apartment door a half minute later, a haggard, dishevelled Clarke followed his grandchildren inside.

"I'm sorry, Maggie. I'm not in a good frame of mind and I don't want to alarm them."

"Don't apologize. Come here." She wrapped her arms around him and kissed him soundly.

He was near tears. "I knew I would spend the morning watching the hands go around on the clock."

"You catch up on the morning news on the television and the kiddies and I will start the pancakes."

She turned the television on then ushered Kelly and Sean into the kitchen. They found some frozen blueberries that weren't too badly covered in frost and mixed them into the batter. Margaret always made her own maple syrup substitute with brown sugar and maple extract. Twenty minutes later, they had the dining room table set and Clarke was sitting at the head of it taking the first bite.

Margaret kept the children chattering about their impending first day of school and Kelly asked if she could borrow the book she and Sean had been looking through the evening before. The conversation continued until finally Margaret gave them the task of cleaning up. "You helped cook the pancakes so that makes you chefs also and the chef always leaves his or her kitchen clean and tidy. I'll show you where the broom is to sweep up as well."

"What are you going to do, Grandma?" Sean didn't let it pass that they were doing all the clean-up.

"I am going to sit and enjoy a cup of coffee with Grandpa."

She had just poured a fresh mug of the brew for Clarke when her doorbell rang. again It was Helen and Gerald. "We're going over to Costco and ... oh, you've got company."

"Come in. Clarke and the kids are here for pancakes."

The haggard appearance of Clarke spoke volumes.

Gerald walked over to sit on a chair near him. "You don't look so great. Are you okay?"

"Kirsten is having surgery this morning and Clarke is waiting to receive word from the hospital."

"What kind of surgery?"

Clarke and Margaret brought the Merciers up to date on Kirsten's state of health.

"You poor dear man." Helen was truly sympathetic to Clarke's concern. "You must be beside yourself with worry."

"It's breaking my heart that I'm not there with her, but I know she'd appreciate that the children are being taken care of."

"I don't think you are in any shape to be travelling down the length of the hemisphere anyway." Gerald voiced his concern. "That's a trip daunting enough for a healthy young person but you aren't long out of the hospital yourself, Clarke. You could end up back in hospital down there with no one to care for you or your daughter then."

"You're talking the truth, I know. I'm just upset over the consequences that's all. My little girl needs me there and her children need me here. I can't be in two places."

Margaret brought coffee for the newcomers and was setting it on the dining room table when Clarke's phone rang. He was absolutely grey when he put it to his ear.

The conversation from their end did not sound great. Clarke slumped farther into the chair he was sitting in with each bit of dialogue from the other end. When he finally closed the connection, his eyes were wet.

"They couldn't complete the surgery. It was too dangerous."

Margaret quickly sat on the arm of the chair and wrapped her arms around him.

"What's the matter, Grandpa? Did something happen to Mom?" Kelly was standing by the dining table with tears running down her cheeks.

Helen and Gerald offered to leave so they could talk among themselves, but Clarke insisted they stay. He called the hospital once more for updates. He was curious if there was any chance she could be brought to Ottawa in the near future.

The doctor on the other end was non-committal. There was nothing more he could tell Clarke until Kirsten had a couple of days of rest after this latest ordeal.

Kelly had grasped Margaret's hand and was hanging on tight. Sean was sitting on the floor by his grandfather. Neither child had said very much but Margaret sensed they were fully aware of the danger their mother was in. Kirsten had even asked her grandfather if it was because of them he couldn't go to get their mother. Clarke explained that even if he could leave them, he was not strong enough to make the trip himself. The other three adults exchanged looks of utter despair.

Gerald and Helen stayed for another hour then left with instructions they were to be notified if there was any change in Kirsten's condition. They said they'd let Olivia and Sarah know what was happening.

The two dropped by again on their way home from shopping. Clarke was on the balcony staring at something in the distance. Margaret and the children were playing gin rummy. At Helen's raised eyebrow, she said, "Apparently, Kirsten called out to her dad while under the anaesthetic. Clarke is just about done in."

Gerald and Helen exchanged a sad look. Clarke noticed them and came inside. Margaret thought she saw Helen nudge Gerald followed by a barely perceivable nod by him in return.

"Is your passport current, Clarke?"

Chapter Thirty-eight

"You would do this for me?" Clarke's question was full of incredulity.

"If it were my daughter down there I would want to be with her. Helen and I talked and we agreed. She'll help Margaret with your grandchildren, who by the way, she now thinks of as her grandchildren, too, while I help you get to your daughter's bedside where you're needed."

Margaret and Clarke both stood open mouthed.

Kelly was the first to reply. "Grandpa, are you going to go help Mom?"

Clarke's mouth was moving but nothing was coming out.

Margaret looked at Helen with an "are you nuts?" kind of expression.

"I can't let you do this." Clarke sat back down on his chair.

"Well, fella, I've travelled many places in this world when I was working aboard ship but I've never been to Peru. I'm sorry it's a tragedy that's taking me there now, but I'm determined. We're both determined." He gestured toward Helen as he spoke.

"Clarke, don't argue." Helen's tone was absolute. "Now, you and Gerald have lots to do. An airplane flight to book and hotel rooms just for starters. Margaret and I can look at the children's school schedules and deal with this end of it later. Let's get moving."

"Grandpa, you *have* to go. Mom needs you. Maybe she'll get

better quicker when she sees you."

"You don't mind if I go away and leave you with Maggie and Helen?

Sean piped up. "Grandpa, whenever I'm sick Mom always makes me feel better when she sits and reads to me. Maybe you can sit and read to her. You're her dad."

"Please, Grandpa. I've been praying for God to find some way for you to go."

"It sounds like a done deal to me. Let's get this show on the road." Gerald prodded.

"It might take a while before Kirsten is able to travel. We may not be able to come back for a couple of weeks."

"If that's the case, I was reading that short term leases on apartments are available at a cheaper rate than a hotel room."

"Maggie?" Clarke looked at Margaret. "You haven't said anything."

"I … I'm dumbfounded." She looked at the children then at her friends and back to Clarke. "I'm worried about you, darling. Are you going to be okay?"

All eyes turned to Clarke.

"I couldn't do it on my own. I know my own weaknesses. However, if Gerald is travelling with me, he can be my legs when mine give out. His brain is operating on all cylinders which I know mine is not." He looked at everyone waiting for his acceptance. "I don't think I could ever live with myself if I didn't accept this opportunity to go and see about bringing my daughter home."

The men couldn't leave as quickly as they had hoped. Clarke had to have medical clearance before he was allowed travel insurance. Legal papers again were needed for Margaret to be named as legal guardian of the children in Clarke's absence.

When these delays first appeared, Margaret felt sorry for Clarke. He was anxious to leave and could have if there were not the children to consider. He told Margaret he knew he had a responsibility to make sure there would be no financial ramifications if he too should happen to need medical care while down there. It was also absolutely necessary that Margaret not be hampered from doing anything for his grandchildren that she might have to do. He was giving her full authority over their care. She felt the weight of these responsibilities fall heavily on her shoulders. However, the knowledge that Clarke would not be travelling alone helped to lighten the load. In a few short weeks he had gone from a young, vibrant sixty-two-year-old to a man whose appearance was that of a failing septuagenarian. She hoped this journey wouldn't take a further toll on his longevity.

Helen and Gerald had left to make their own plans. The late afternoon had quickly become late evening.

"Maggie, will you come with me while I try to get these children settled down? We'll go in my car and you can return home by cab. My mind is going in a thousand different directions."

"Of course, they are excited about your going. I think it's a big relief to them to know their mother won't be alone down there any longer."

"It will be a big relief for me also."

Once the kids were settled into their beds, Margaret made tea for Clarke and her. She placed it on the dining room table, but he motioned for her to put it on the coffee table instead. "I want you to sit by me."

He sipped his tea and placed the cup back on its saucer before taking Margaret's hand. "Everything has happened so quickly, you and I have not had a chance to talk. What are your thoughts, Maggie? Are you okay with me going? You've hardly had an opportunity to think about your role in all of this. It's all been about me again. And Kirsten."

Margaret took her time answering.

"Clarke, I don't think I've been very secretive about my love for you. I want whatever you want. Your grandchildren are the most important people in my life next to you. They miss their parents badly, especially their mother. If you, Superman, can go down there and encourage her to recover enough to be brought back here, we will all be ecstatic. With Helen's help, I will take very good care of my grandchildren no matter how long it takes. My only real concern is your stamina. Now I'm being selfish, but I don't want to lose you."

Clarke looked down at his clasped hands for a few moments.

"You've segued into what I have to say, to ask, and made it easier for me to find the words."

He took a deep breath before searching her eyes.

"I can sense how deep my feelings must have been for you before my accident. I think it's important for you to know that. But it's my feelings for you now that matter. Maggie, I love you. I love everything about you. I love your tenderness, your compassion, your face, your hair, your body, your smile." He stroked her face, her hair and her shoulders as he spoke. "I love your soul, your integrity, your devotion. I love that you love me. I especially love that you can give yourself so unselfishly and unconditionally to me, to *my* needs and those of my family." He smiled almost awkwardly.

"There I go again. Everything is I, I, I. Just one more I." He took her hands. "I want you to marry me. Right away. Before I go."

He was met with silence.

"Maggie?"

"I would love to marry you, but I'm worried you might be asking me out of a state of duress. You said yourself your brain isn't operating on all cylinders."

"I'm asking you because I love you. I want you to be my wife.

I want to make love to you. I want to know when I come back we will live together as man and wife. My God, Maggie, having you so close every single day and night, it's been darn near impossible for me not to want you in my bed."

"So you're after my body." She smiled somewhat coyly.

"Yes, woman, I'm after your body. I'm after everything about you. I don't like that we're not sharing a roof. I hate that you go home or I go home to our own beds each night. I hate having to call you on the phone just to hear your voice."

"There you go. Everything is about your wants again."

She laughed at his startled look.

"Don't you think I have some wants and needs also? As luck would have it, they coincide with yours, so yes, Clarke, I will marry you."

The grin on his face was quickly erased by her next words.

"But not until you come back from Peru."

Chapter Thirty-nine

"Why do you want to wait if you're sure you want to marry him?"

"When we get married, I don't want any shadows over us. I want him of sound mind. That's not to mean I doubt his sanity but stop and think. What if his memory tells him that he didn't want marriage, only companionship. What if uncertainty or doubt accompanies his full cognisance? What if, when he's stronger of both body and mind, he has questions about being taken advantage of while not so healthy?"

"You don't trust him?"

Margaret sensed that Helen was having difficulty understanding her thinking but it didn't matter. Her mind was made up.

"I do trust him. I know that he had strong feelings for me before his accident and he has strong feelings for me now. I just want to make sure that those feelings are continuous — one and the same, so to speak."

"Margaret, a blind person could see the love he has for you. He can't keep his eyes off you. Love emanates from every pore in that man's body."

"I will marry him when he returns."

Helen shook her head but didn't argue.

The legal paperwork was done. The insurance was put in place. It proved very expensive but necessary. The flights were booked and hotel rooms secured near the hospital in Lima.

Margaret had been to the school and was duly registered as their guardian and first contact. Helen's name was included as alternate contact. Clarke had expressed his disappointment at not being allowed to register Margaret as their grandmother. It was the evening before their departure and the children were excited that their grandfather would be with their mother the next day.

"Grandpa, make sure you tell Mom that I'm going to play soccer at school. She always liked that I played." Sean had been giving a list of things he wanted his mother to know.

"And don't forget to tell her that Grandma makes sure we both brush and floss our teeth every night. Mom used to get upset whenever Sean tried to sneak into bed without doing that." Kelly made a face at her brother.

"Speaking of which, it's time for both of you to do just that. We have to be at the airport early. I'll make sure you do it tonight so that I can tell her I saw it with my own eyes." He patted each on the bum as they begrudgingly made their way to the bathroom.

Margaret emptied the dishwasher and put everything away. By the time Clarke had the children tucked into bed she was sitting down to finally read the morning newspaper. There had been no time during the day.

"Stay with me. I can't bear to have you leave me alone in my bed tonight."

"But the children …"

"The children will be delighted to see you in the morning."

"But you're an ordained min—"

"I know what I am, Maggie. I am a man. A man in love with a beautiful, caring, adorable, God-fearing woman who is going to share my bed tonight. I tried to make you my wife but you would have no part of that. So if I'm going to be condemned to hell for my thoughts, I may as well go there for my actions as well."

He took her hand and pulled her to stand in front of him. He gently tucked her beautiful silver hair behind her ear then lifted her chin and kissed her gently. She leaned into the kiss, her heart dancing pirouettes inside her chest. He slid his arm around her waist and pulled her body against his.

"Come." He beckoned with his head for her to follow him.

❦ ❦ ❦

It was time to leave for the airport. Gerald's van was large enough to seat all six of them with just enough room for the luggage in the very back. Clarke never let go of Margaret's hand as they made their way down Bronson Avenue to the airport.

As it was an international flight, the men had to be at the airport hours ahead of their actual departure time. Arrangements had been made for Clarke to have wheelchair assistance through all the flight changes at all the airports. Gerald loaded their bags onto a cart and pushed it inside. Sean pulled his grandfather's carry-on behind him. The children sat on either side of their grandfather once the larger bags had been checked through. They chose chairs that overlooked part of the runway.

The time finally came for Gerald and Clarke to go through security. The children gave their grandfather long teary hugs and clung to his pant legs while he tried to kiss Margaret.

"Hey kids, don't I get any hugs?" Gerald came to the rescue.

"I will call anytime there's something to report." Clarke smiled. "I'll also call when I just need to hear your voice. Take care of yourself. Don't let the children wear you down." He put his arms around her and kissed her soundly. "Just remember I love you, Maggie."

He pulled her close again and whispered in her ear. "Thank you for last night."

She was crying visibly and couldn't get any words out. Finally, after a deep breath, "I was a damn fool, Clarke. I should have married you. Please, please look after yourself."

One last hug for each of the children and he was through

the gate.

Margaret had not stayed the night. Clarke had surprised her with the tenderness and passion of his lovemaking. He had been careful of satisfying her needs, taking his time making sure she enjoyed it as much as he did. She was not left wanting for more but something inside her warned her against allowing the children to find them in bed in the morning. Maybe she was old-fashioned or maybe it was because of the excellent moral standard he had set for his children and grandchildren, she had insisted on going home.

"Well, kids, who wants to go for pancakes?" Helen didn't give any of them time to cry.

She took them to Cora's. The portions were good and there was always fresh fruit on the plate. After breakfast, Helen offered to show the kids her condo in the same building as Margaret's.

"I'll give you an hour to yourself then we have to decide who's doing what and when next week. Olivia and Sarah have offered to help out also."

"Will Grandpa and Uncle Gerald be there yet?" Kelly had been quiet on the ride from the restaurant.

"No, sweetie. They won't arrive until after you're in bed tonight. It's a long way down there. You must know where it is from looking at your Atlas or globe." Helen knew they were old enough to figure the distance out.

"But they've been gone for two hours."

"No. We've been gone from the airport for two hours but their plane hadn't left yet." She looked at her watch. "They've only been in the air for about one hour. Then they have to stop and change planes in Toronto. I think they're on the ground there for a couple of hours then they have to fly all the way down through the United States and Mexico to Panama. I think that part of the trip takes about five hours. After waiting for a couple hours again they will get on a different plane to fly to Lima. That flight is about four or five hours. So you see it takes a long time to get there. Both men will be very tired by the time they arrive and get into their hotel room. That's why Uncle Gerald went too. He will help taking care of their carry-on bags and getting your grandpa from one part of the airport to another and looking after the transportation from the airport in Lima. It's a very tiring journey for young people let alone a couple of men in their sixties, especially when one of them is physically handicapped."

"Wow. I didn't think about it taking that long. Why can't the same plane fly all the way there?"

"Because it would run out of gas, silly." Sean shook his head and looked at Helen. "Girls don't know anything about airplanes."

"I do so."

"Okay, now. Do you want to see some pictures of my grandchildren? You might get to meet them one day."

"Where do they live?" Kelly turned her back on her brother.

"Two of them live in Kingston and one lives in Vancouver." She kept them occupied until Margaret knocked on the door. A few minutes later Olivia and Sarah arrived. They worked out a schedule for the following week which included the start of school.

"Ready to go home?" Margaret had two suitcases to take to Clarke's place as she would be spending most of her nights there. This was timely since the renovations to her kitchen would be starting soon.

"Will you be okay, Margaret?"

"Yes. We have some things to keep us busy today. Call if you hear from Gerald and I'll do the same with any news from Clarke."

"Did you get a cell phone?"

"That's on my list of things to do tomorrow. I know I'll need one now."

Margaret left with the two children in tow to get her car and start on the next leg of her journey. Not really on her home turf, but close. With three friends to spell her off, she would get some days off and even time to come home weekly.

Chapter Forty

"Margaret, you have to call the school. Sean says he had to go sit in the principal's office today."

"What? What did he do?"

"He said some boy was calling him names in the schoolyard so he pushed him down." Olivia was upset.

"No one called me. Shouldn't they let the parents know when there's a fight on school property?" Margaret was at the beauty salon and Olivia had taken a turn at waiting for the children to get off the school bus then had taken them upstairs to Clarke's condo.

"I'll question Sean a little more when I get home then deal with the school tomorrow."

It upset her that someone might be bullying Sean and she wanted it nipped in the bud. He was an active child but well-behaved and polite. Never having to deal with teachers and schools before, she had to wonder what the protocol was. *Well, I guess I'll find out.*

She did find out that the other boy had spent time in the dreaded principal's office also. Olivia had offered to go to the school with her and give the principal a piece of her mind. Margaret declined the offer. The thought of Olivia as a defensive parent or grandparent was more than she could ever have pictured. The children had won the hearts of every one of them. From having only one grandfather and a distant aunt, they now had two grandparents, three great-aunts and one great-uncle.

In the week the men had been in Lima, Kirsten had undergone two surgeries and been taken off the coma-inducing drugs. The pain medication was quite strong though and she spent most of the time sleeping. She had opened her eyes several times and recognized her father but was too weak to remain awake long enough to have a conversation. It was the weakness that was keeping her from being released. She was nowhere near strong enough to endure the long flights home.

"It's enough that she smiled at me and I felt a slight squeeze when I held her hand. Maggie, I'm so happy I came. She knows her daddy is here. One of the doctors said her breathing has relaxed a little since I arrived. Gerald stays with me quite a bit so she hears our voices. I read to her also."

"How's your own strength? The long hours at the hospital must be very tiring for you, Clarke."

"I'm fine. Gerald is like a mother hen, hovering all the time. He makes sure I take my medication and that I rest with my leg up several times a day. He's not you, but he tries hard."

Margaret could hear Gerald's voice in the background followed by a laugh.

"Oh, we found a small, inexpensive apartment hotel not far from the hospital that we can rent by the week. It even has a small stove and refrigerator, so we can fix a few hot meals and not have to pay for restaurant food all the time. It's cleaned thoroughly and sheets are changed once each week. We'll move into it tomorrow. Hopefully we'll know a little more by that time when Kirsten might be able to go home."

"It sounds like everything is falling into place there. I'm so glad that Gerald was able to go with you. Has he had a chance to do any sightseeing?"

"He's only walked about a bit but tomorrow he's going to the Larco Museum and in a few days we may both go to one of the old churches. A lot of the tourist attractions involve many sets of stairs, so I'll leave those for him to tour on his own. He also wants to see some of the waterfront."

"It sounds like there's a lot for him to see and do."

"Now, let me talk to my grandchildren for a little bit."

❣ ❣ ❣

It was well past midnight when her cell phone rang. She recognized the foreign area code.

"Do you have bright turquoise matching pants and jacket?" His voice was so soft it was almost a whisper.

"Yes, I wore that outfit a couple of times in the late spring before the summer got too hot."

Then the realization hit. "I haven't worn it since your accident. I didn't even take it to Hamilton with me."

"I was lying here in bed thinking about you when something went off in my brain like a camera flash. For a split second I saw you walking out a door wearing it."

Margaret didn't know what to say.

"Maggie, darling. You looked so beautiful."

"I'll wear it to the airport when the three of you come home." She tried unsuccessfully to hide the tremor in her voice.

"I love you."

"I love you, too. Good night, darling."

She cried herself to sleep.

The next day Kelly was sent home from school with head lice.

"How in hell did she get head lice?" It was Sarah's day to have the children after school, so Margaret had taken advantage of her day off to go to Wakefield in Quebec with Olivia for lunch and then an hour at the spa.

When the school called on her cell phone, Margaret relayed the message to Sarah.

"What do I do? Do we have to fumigate the apartment?"

"The school secretary said Kelly will have a note with her

about a product to treat her with. It's an over-the-counter cream or something that has to be put on her hair. If you can pick it up for me at the drug store, I'll be home in a short while and I can do the treatment. I don't think the place has to be fumigated but I'm not sure. I never thought to ask."

By the time Margaret arrived home, Kelly had a towel on her head and Sarah had stripped the girl's bed and placed a load of Kelly's things in the washer.

"Don't look so surprised. I'm not exactly helpless you know. Once I spoke with the woman at the school I realized it's no big deal." Sarah patted Kelly on the shoulder. "She wasn't the only one, poor girl."

"One of the girl's in my class asked to use my brush the other day after recess. I didn't want to but she's nice and I didn't want to hurt her feelings. It ended up both her and her sister have head lice." Kelly shrugged her shoulders as if it was nothing serious.

"How did anyone find out?"

"Someone was at the school today doing routine checks. My teacher said there was an outbreak in the school."

"What about your brother? Have you used his pillow or shared your brush with him?"

"Of course not. I don't want his germs on me." She shuddered as if just the thought of him touching her stuff was horrifying.

"Put your hairbrush in a plastic bag, seal it and throw it in the garbage."

While Sarah went downstairs to get Sean from the bus Margaret stripped his bed, vacuumed the mattress and put fresh sheets on it. *So much for my relaxing afternoon at the spa.*

When Margaret's cell phone rang shortly after supper she didn't recognize the screen. "What is this?" Then it stopped ringing.

"What's the matter, Grandma?" Kelly sat beside Margaret.

"I'm not sure." Before she could say anything more it rang again.

Kelly looked at it. "It's Grandpa. He's facetiming."

"He's what?"

Kelly took the phone from her and slid her finger across the display. Instantly Clarke's face showed on the screen.

"Hi, Grandpa." She started to cry.

Sean whooped and turned Kelly's hands so the phone faced him.

"Hi Grandpa. Are you still in Peru? Is Mom getting better? When will you guys be home?"

"Whoa! Slow down. I'm still in Peru and your mother is showing signs of getting better and we're not sure yet when we'll be home. Soon, I hope. How are you?"

Before Kelly could speak, Sean continued. "I'm good but Kelly got head lice at school."

"Sean! Stop it. Why did you say that?" Kelly pulled the phone beyond his reach and looked at her grandfather. "Aunt Sarah and Grandma treated my hair and I'm okay now. Are you with Mom? Can we see her?"

"I'm glad to hear you're both okay. Head lice, eh? I guess that's something to be expected when you go to school. I'll let you see your mother. She's sleeping right now and remember that she was badly injured so don't be frightened by how frail she looks. The doctor says she is doing well. Then I want you to give the phone to Grandma so I can see her and talk to her."

The view on the screen shifted and soon it was focused on a thin woman with dark shadows under her closed eyes. Kelly started to cry again and Sean commented, "She looks old."

"You'd look old if you went through what she's gone through. But now you can see that she's still weak and will need lots of time to get better. We don't want to move her until we're sure she can safely make the long trip home."

"Grandpa, will you kiss her right now and tell her that's from me?"

Kelly watched as her grandfather gave her mother a kiss on the cheek and said, "That's from Kelly and here's one from Sean." He placed another soft kiss on the sleeping woman's cheek.

"I think she blinked in her sleep so she knows I kissed her for you. Now throw me a kiss and let me talk to Grandma."

Kelly kissed her fingers then blew towards the phone in the traditional manner. Sean kissed his fingers them wound up like a pitcher and tossed the kiss toward the phone. Clarke responded to them in kind before the phone was given to Margaret.

"It's a good thing Kelly was here because I had no idea what to do with the phone. You might have been attempting to reach me this way all day. You know me and cell phones aren't best friends yet." Margaret smiled into the phone.

The children went back to the kitchen to finish their homework.

"I'm glad I caught you all together. I won't keep the connection open too long though. I just wanted to see all of you and know you haven't torn your hair out yet." He grinned. "Head lice, eh? Good lord, are you going to survive another week or two?"

"It wasn't me that had to deal with it. It was Sarah that was on duty this afternoon and I have to say she showed great patience. How is Kirsten?"

He moved the phone again so that Margaret could see his daughter in the background. "It's slow going but at least she's remaining stable, not sliding backwards. The doctor feels that if she continues to show signs of improvement in the next week, he'll assess her condition again. We may have to pay to have a trained nurse travel with us. We have to get approval from each of the airlines involved and carry the necessary medical paperwork. We'll know more in a few days."

"Clarke, I can't find the words to tell you how excited I am that you remembered my turquoise pant suit. I hope this is the beginning of your memory return."

"Me too. I want to remember every single moment we spent together. I'm somewhat jealous that you have those memories and I don't but I'm getting little splashes of recollections here and there. Are you keeping well, love?"

"Yes. Everyone is. The children are doing well. I know Kelly misses her mother more with each passing day but she's remaining strong. Sean seems to be adapting to the situation a little better. I'm surprised neither mention their father anymore. Is there any news on that front?"

"Nothing. It's as if he's gone off the map — literally and figuratively. Once we have Kirsten safely home I'll renew and increase my efforts into finding out where he might be. I'm in touch with the Mission officials almost daily and they are continuing their efforts but nothing new is surfacing. They are responsible for his well-being so it's not like no one is looking."

"That's good. I know this call or facetime or whatever it's called must be costing a fortune so I'll throw you a kiss also." She mimicked Sean's pitch.

"I love you, Maggie. It makes my hospital vigil here a lot easier knowing you are taking care of my family there. You are an amazing woman." She could hear him take another breath. "I love that you are keeping my bed warm. I picture your beautiful face on my pillow each night. Good night, my love." He kissed the air near the screen and closed the connection.

Chapter Forty-one

"Mrs. McFarland, we simply cannot allow those in attendance at our sporting events to use foul language. Miss Kovacs owes the official an apology and she will not be allowed to watch any more track meets." The school principal called Margaret after Olivia had been asked to leave the stands after a verbal outburst from her.

Olivia and Margaret had gone to watch Sean compete in the tryouts for the school track team. Olivia disagreed with a measurement taken in one of the boy's long jumps.

"So I called the man an asshole. Why not? That's exactly what he is. He's prejudiced because Sean is a newcomer to the school. Anyone could see that Sean landed inches past where that blind man put the marker. He deserved to be called out on it."

Margaret shook her head. "Olivia, it's an elementary school meet. It's not college try-outs."

"So that asshole should be allowed to get away with it just because these kids are young? This could shape how far they go in school athletics. If Sean doesn't make this team he may be dejected enough not to try out for anything — ever. He'll lose chances for scholarships."

"Sean also has to learn about sportsmanship, discipline and respect for authority. Even if the man was wrong, and I'm not saying he was, the boy has to accept that as part of the learning experience. If Sean felt the measurement wasn't accurate he could have questioned it politely. Or taken it like a man, practised more then jumped better next time. Those teachers and coaches are donating their time, for the most part."

"Okay, I'll apologize but not because I think that guy was right. I'll do it for Sean. I don't want to get him in trouble with the school or coaches."

"Thank you."

❦ ❦ ❦

The next few days slid by without any incidents. Kelly appeared to be withdrawing more and more into a shell. Several attempts by Margaret to draw her out only seemed to make it worse.

"You've been very quiet these past few days, Kelly. I can understand that you must miss your parents terribly, but is there anything else on your mind? Are you having any problems at school?"

"No. I'm fine."

"Would you like to do anything special this weekend?"

"Not really."

"Maybe we can go for a drive down to Prescott or Brockville for lunch on Saturday."

"Okay."

"Do you have all your homework done?"

"Yes."

"Are you upset with me about something?"

"No." With that she walked into her bedroom.

Clarke called again that evening on the landline. He talked to the children first as always then asked to speak to Margaret. Kirsten's medications had been reduced slightly and she appeared to remain comfortable. She was breathing well, and her blood pressure and pulse were stable.

"The doctor said if she doesn't have any setbacks over the next two days, we can start making arrangements to bring her home. He'll be ready to sign the release papers for the airline at that time. It might take a few days for everything to be done because space has to be prepared for her. The hospital in Ottawa has to be notified also so they can prepare to receive her. My doctor is taking care of the paperwork at that end. I didn't tell the children because I don't want to get their hopes up in case there's a delay for any reason."

"Clarke, that's wonderful. I will be so relieved when all of you arrive at the airport. I am so worried about your own health. It looks like all our prayers will soon be answered." Margaret was tearing up and her voice broke.

"Kelly seemed quiet on the phone tonight. Is she okay?"

"Strange you should mention that. I noticed her reticence also and questioned her about it. She says she's fine but I'm wondering if the strain of everything that's happened is finally taking its toll on her."

"That must be difficult for you, Maggie."

"Not difficult, just sad. I want her to be well. I thought she had been dealing with everything but maybe she was just hiding it well. I won't put any pressure on her and pray she pulls herself out of it or at least opens up to me about it."

"How is she doing in school?"

"The few things she's brought home that needed signing look really good. She's receiving good marks and her teacher's comments are excellent. It's only been two weeks."

"That's good at least.

"Sean tells me he didn't make the track team. He seemed a little disappointed."

"Yes, he was. He was very close so maybe next year. I've suggested he join a youth bowling league and he's considering it."

Margaret kept her fingers crossed that Sean hadn't said anything about Olivia's outburst at the tryout.

"And you, Maggie, how are you doing?"

"With so much help from all my friends, I have less to do than I ever did. I think each is trying to outdo the other. I've not had to buy anything for school lunches. They keep bringing or sending cookies, fruit, juice boxes, varieties of cheese, muffins and cold cuts. It's only mid-September and Sarah has already offered to take them shopping for winter jackets and ski suits. Olivia has offered to pay for ski lessons for both of them. I know Helen misses Gerald because she comes over often in the evening just to pass the time."

"Gerald misses her, too. Every time he visits a tourist attraction or ventures into another section of the city, he comments on how much Helen would have enjoyed seeing it. He wants to bring her here so she can see everything that he's seen." After a moment of silence, "I miss you terribly, Maggie. I think about you all day and all night. If it wasn't for needing you there, I would have you here in a minute."

"Well, darling, I *am* needed here and you are needed *there* so we have to put our wants and needs on the back burner for just a short time longer. Besides my kitchen is in the middle of renovations, another reason why I must stay close to home."

"I hope we'll get married as soon as I return. We can take a honeymoon later, but I can't wait for you to be my wife. I love you so much."

"We will. I want it, too."

Two days later the phone rang in the middle of the day.

"We'll be arriving late on Monday night. The hospital-to-hospital air transfer is being completed as we speak. Gerald has been pulling a few strings with people he knows. Apparently, there's a golfing buddy of his who has a position of power and was able to get things approved quickly. The doctor here has assured us Kirsten will be sedated and made safe for transport. Once we're in Panama, a smaller plane will take us to Miami and then we'll be on a direct flight home."

"That's only three days away. Oh, Clarke, I am so happy for all of you. I can hardly wait for the children to come home from school so I can tell them."

Margaret burst into tears as she placed the phone back on its base. Her doorbell rang.

Helen. She'll be happy that Gerald will be home soon too.

When she opened the door, it wasn't Helen on the other side but another neighbour, Stella Jacobson. She and the others had treated Stella badly a couple of years previously. Thinking she was man crazy, they had made unkind jokes about her and subsequently had caused major problems between Helen and Gerald. It was Margaret and Stella that had been the instigators in one particular set of events. Their suspicions had been unfounded, and, in the end, Stella had turned out to be a good friend to Helen and a respected neighbour to the others.

"Margaret, I only stopped by to apologize for not being around to offer my help." She had a covered plate in her hands. "I thought the children might enjoy some cupcakes I made today."

"Come in, Stella. No need for apologies. I know you are busy with your business." She took the platter of baked goods and motioned Stella to a chair.

"How are the children? And how is their mother?"

"The children are doing well. I'll be leaving shortly for Clarke's place to meet the school bus. I only came home to pick up a couple of things and approve some flooring samples."

"I noticed your car in the parkade and hoped I would catch you here."

"This is so nice of you. You are such a good baker, the children will enjoy them for sure. I had just hung up the phone when you rang the doorbell. It looks like Clarke and Gerald will be returning home at the beginning of next week. Clarke's daughter is deemed well enough to be transferred to the hospital here. I believe she'll be going to the Ottawa General."

"That is such good news, Margaret. From what I can gather you've been a caregiver of one kind or another for most of the summer. I'm so sorry that you've had such a chain of bad luck."

"Well, I consider myself the lucky one since it's not been me in the hospital. Poor Clarke. He woke up from a coma only to find out his daughter was in one. It's been like living in a soap opera. I hope once they arrive here it will be the beginning of better things for everyone."

"I hope so too, Margaret. You're a good person to take on all that you have. I won't keep you. I don't want you to miss the school bus. The children will be happy to have their mother and grandfather home, I'm sure."

"Yes, they will. Thank you for stopping in, Stella. We'll have to get together once things return to normal around here. I'll have everyone over for a celebration once Clarke is up to it."

"Their return home will be cause for major celebration. I'll be delighted to come and especially to meet Clarke."

Margaret leaned in as if sharing a secret. "The celebration may in the form of an engagement party rather than a welcome home event. Clarke and I hope to be married soon."

Stella's face lit up. "Oh, Margaret, that is fantastic. I am so happy for you."

The women hugged and Stella left.

Chapter Forty-two

Sean threw his baseball glove into the air and knocked a crystal candy dish off an end table. The carpeting saved it from breaking into a hundred pieces. Helen didn't scold as she picked it up. She knew the boy was excited by the news of his mother's imminent arrival home.

Kelly cried through her smile. "You mean they're really coming?"

"Barring any unforeseen circumstances, they should be here very late on Monday."

"Why do they have to wait so long? If Mom is better why can't they leave tomorrow?" Sean's impatience showed in his question.

"A lot of paperwork and preparation has to be done before they can leave. It's not easy to bring a person from a hospital in one country in one hemisphere to another hospital in another country in another hemisphere. It's not the same as merely bringing her across the American and Canadian border. Plus, the airline company doesn't want to be held responsible if she should get sick while in the air."

"Do you think she'll get sick?" A deep frown had formed across Sean's forehead.

"No, I don't. The hospital wouldn't let her go if they were worried but even healthy people sometimes get sick on planes. The airline company needs both your grandfather and a doctor to sign papers that they won't hold the airline responsible if she does. It's all just paperwork, honey, but it has to be done and it takes time."

"I'm happy I'll finally get to see her and touch her." Kelly looked wistfully at the picture of her mother and father on the mantle.

When Margaret went to Kelly's room later to say night time prayers with her she found the girl sobbing uncontrollably.

"Kelly, dear, what's got you so upset? Are you worried about your mother's flight home?"

Kelly wiped her face with a tissue and it took a minute or two for her to bring her crying under control.

"Grandma, I am worried about my dad. If Mom and Grandpa come home, he has no one down there to worry about him. What's going to happen? He'll be all by himself and what if he needs someone to help him." Getting it all out set her off on another bawling session.

Margaret's heart ached for the girl. She pulled her into a hug. "There, there, little one." She rocked the girl while cradling her in her arms and let her cry. "Shh. You go ahead and let all the hurt and worry come out in those tears. Just get rid of it all."

She spent the next hour soothing and explaining what Clarke had said about the police and the Mission people continuing the search and not giving up. They recited some encouraging prayers together. Finally, the sobbing slowed to the odd hiccup and then disappeared altogether.

Margaret finally knew what had been bothering Kelly. All the love and care and rescue efforts were directed toward her mother, for which she was grateful, but it had seemed to her that everyone had forgotten about her father. She pictured him lying injured in the jungle somewhere feeling all alone and thinking nobody cared. It was sadness that had been building in her heart. As Margaret laid the young girl back down on her pillow and tucked the sheet around her, she couldn't help remembering the walls in

Kelly's bedroom full of jungle trees, grass and animals. They had brought a rope with stuffed monkeys hanging from it and hung it in the room she was currently using as her own. Kelly had told Margaret of her intentions to work in the jungle when she grew up.

I think you've chosen the right career path young lady. However this all plays out, that jungle will be your solace.

She kissed the still-damp cheek and tip-toed out of the room.

Chapter Forty-three

Margaret, Clarke, Helen and Gerald talked several times over the next two days. On Sunday evening Clarke told Margaret he would try to text her from the airport before they took off in the morning, but he couldn't promise.

Margaret had debated keeping Kelly and Sean home from school but decided the day might go by more quickly for them in the classroom where they had to concentrate on lessons. In her heart she knew they probably would be watching the clock and wondering where their mother was, how much closer to home she was with each passing minute.

Helen called Margaret mid-morning and said she was coming over. Shortly after lunch, the school secretary called to say that Sean was complaining of being sick and could someone come and get him. Margaret said she would pick him and his sister up together and bring them home. The teacher and principal had been made aware of the situation because Margaret had anticipated keeping them both at home on Tuesday on the chance they might be allowed to see their mother in the hospital.

The two women were just as wound up as the children were. They had a mid-afternoon tea party then played Scrabble for several hours. At six o'clock, Gerald called Helen to let them know they had arrived in Miami, Florida, and that Kirsten was doing well. She was showing no signs of trauma or anxiety. The nurse was travelling with them right through to Ottawa. They would leave within the hour and arrive in Ottawa about one o'clock in the morning.

Olivia and Sarah arrived about a half hour later with an array of cartons of Chinese take-out for everyone. They had volunteered to stay with the children so that Margaret and Helen could go to the airport to pick up their men who would have to come through customs while a ground ambulance would take Kirsten to the Ottawa General. They would all go to the hospital and attend to Kirsten's admission and see her settled for the night.

At midnight the women couldn't sit any longer and they made their way to the airport.

"I thought we may as well sit here and drink coffee and at least let Olivia and Sarah get some sleep." Helen looked around at the few people sitting in the waiting area then back at her friend.

"You changed your clothes. I like that colour of blue on you."

Margaret smiled. She hadn't mentioned Clarke's window of memory to anyone. She was afraid to hope it was the start of its healing and didn't want to jinx anything. They chatted and had a second laugh about Olivia being kicked out of Sean's track meet.

"Poor Clarke. He may be embarrassed at some of the things that have happened in his absence."

"Margaret, I get the feeling that Clarke isn't as straight-laced as we all thought he was. I think he can enjoy a good laugh as well as anyone. He'll see the humour in these incidents."

"I suppose you're right."

Before she could say anything more, the flight arrival was announced over the loud speaker.

It was about half an hour before the men came off the elevator. Clarke was in a wheelchair and quite pale. He had his canes across his knees and Gerald was pushing him. He looked much older than his age. Margaret wiped away her tears before he saw them.

"Maggie, you look just as I remembered you." He stood and pulled her to him. He was whispering in her ear. "You look exactly like you did the last time I saw you in that suit. If anything, you are even more lovely."

It was a good thing the wheelchair was behind him because he collapsed into it. Frightened, Margaret knelt in front of him. "Are you all right? You must be completely done in."

"I am tired, love, but I think seeing you standing here meeting me just as I met you at the Hamilton airport so long ago, I'm just overwhelmed."

"You mean you remember ... everything?"

"Yes. While Gerald was pushing me toward you everything came back. I remember everything. I'm so sorry. I have been such a burden on you."

She stood and leaned over to kiss him on the top of his head. "Let's get to the hospital before you collapse again."

The ambulance had arrived well ahead of them, but all the necessary paperwork was with her and the nurse. By the time the group had parked and gone through the emergency entrance, they found Kirsten had already been taken to a room in the ICU and was presently being examined by a team of doctors.

They waited another two hours before a doctor about the same age as they were came out to the waiting room. They were told Kirsten had come through the long trip without too much trauma. She had already been through a CT Scan and would be having an MRI early in the morning. For now, they were just going to let her rest. Decisions as to her care and treatment would be made some time in the next day or two. For now, they would be allowed a five minute visit with her and then he advised them all to go home and get some rest themselves.

The nurse who had accompanied Kirsten was dismissed and her accommodations and return home were all arranged. Clarke conveyed to her how grateful he was for the high level of care she had given Kirsten during the flights and transfers.

Helen drove to Clarke's condo and Gerald helped him carry his bags up. It was a given that Margaret would be staying with him. Olivia and Sarah left after many hugs and kisses and tears were exchanged. Margaret agreed to call them later in the day when they had more information.

It was almost dawn by the time Margaret slid into the bed beside Clarke. He turned to her and placed an arm around her before he fell into a dead sleep. She pulled his hand to her lips and kissed his fingers before her eyes closed and her breathing slowed as well.

Chapter Forty-four

"Grandpa. Grandpa, you're home. Can we go see Mom?"

"Yes, Grandpa, is she okay? Can we go to the hospital?"

If the shouting didn't wake them, the bouncing of the mattress from two jumping children certainly would have.

"Careful, kids. You'll fall on your grandfather."

"That's okay. What time is it?" Clarke rolled to look at the clock. The digital readout told him it was 8:15 A.M. "Stop jumping and let me sit up."

He sat up and slid his one foot into a slipper. "Now let's go put some coffee on and I'll tell you all about our trip home and how well your mother is doing."

"It looks like Grandma's gonna do the dishes this morning!" Sean jumped and ran through the bedroom door ahead of everyone.

Kelly was hot on her grandfather's heels rhyming off all the questions she needed answers to.

Margaret waited until the room was clear before she rose and wrapped herself in her housecoat that had been hanging on the hook behind the door. *How handy that my things were already here.*

In the kitchen, Clarke already had the coffee brewing and the children were in the process of pouring orange juice into four glasses. Margaret took a container of muffins from the freezer and placed them in the microwave to thaw and warm.

Once they were all seated around the dining room table,

Clarke proceeded to tell the children how difficult it had been for their mother to reach Ottawa. He started with her sedation and transfer from her bed to an ambulance gurney. It took him almost an hour, answering questions as he went along, before he could tell of their arrival at the airport and then how he had caught up with their mother again at the Ottawa General Hospital.

"Can we go see her Grandpa?" Kelly placed her hand on his arm. Her eyes were wet with tears.

"I will phone the hospital in an hour or so to find out how she spent the night. They were going to run some tests on her this morning to see where they would start with her rehabilitation and subsequent surgeries. They said not to call before mid-morning because they won't be able to tell us anything until at least then. Sean, if you get my phone from beside my bed I'll show you some pictures of her in the plane and at the hospital here."

They saw a picture of her on the gurney in her room in Lima just prior to leaving by land ambulance for the airport and then a couple from inside the plane and again on the tarmac in Florida just before being boarded on the final leg of their flight home. There were several that included the young Peruvian nurse who had accompanied them.

"Is the nurse still with her? Can we meet her?" Kelly was studying the girl in the photo.

"No, I believe she was catching a flight just about now to go back home. I have her e-mail address so we can send her a picture of your mom when she's awake and able to smile for the camera."

"What's her name?"

"It's funny sometimes how life is. Her name is Margarita."

"That sounds like Grandma's name." Sean grinned.

"It is Grandma's name in Spanish."

"Margaret – Margarita. That's cool."

"Now, why don't we get cleaned up and put some clothes on

then you can tell me all about school and whatever else you've been doing since I left."

By the time they were finished telling him about their school, teachers and activities they had signed up for, it was almost eleven o'clock. Sean had been glancing at Margaret all through the telling. When they finally took a break and Clarke went to get the number and extension to call to reach the right desk at the hospital, Sean came and gave Margaret a hug. "Thank you for not telling Grandpa about me getting in a fight at school."

"That's not a story he needs to know about unless it happens again. If it does, then no doubt it will be the teacher or principal telling him." She patted his head.

"It won't happen again, I promise."

They sat in the living room and listened while Clarke spoke with a couple of different people at the hospital. He had set the phone on speaker so that everyone could hear both ends of the conversation. They learned that Kirsten had spent a peaceful night only waking up once. She was slowly showing signs of the heavy sedation wearing off but had yet to open her eyes. She had responded to stimuli with movements and facial expressions. They had done several tests including an MRI. The family was welcome to visit her briefly later in the afternoon but only one adult and one child at a time and for no longer than ten minutes each visit.

That news evoked a couple of whoops from the children. Margaret quickly put her finger to her lips in an attempt to quieten them. She whispered, "You don't want them to think you're going to be loud and boisterous up at the hospital." They nodded knowingly and sat quiet for the rest of the conversation.

Margaret relayed the news from the hospital to Helen and Gerald and they, in turn, called the other two women.

"How's your new bed, Sean? Are you sleeping comfortably in it? Spiderman hasn't booted you out of it or anything?"

The conversation was kept light until it was time to go. When they arrived at the unit, Clarke begged them to allow both children in for two minutes then they would leave and return one at a time. He couldn't find it in his heart to allow one the first visit over the other.

When they approached her sleeping form on the bed, Kelly gasped and drew back. "She looks dead." The tears ran down her cheeks as she whispered the words.

"She's not, Kell. Look, her chest is moving." Sean took the last few steps almost at a run.

Kelly slowly went to the other side of the bed and gazed down at the thin face of her mother.

"Can I touch her?" She looked at her grandfather with total sadness.

"Of course you can. Each of you can take a hand."

Kelly reached for the closest one which had the oxygen clamp on it. "Mom, it's me, Kelly. Can you hear me?"

"I'm here too, Mom." Sean held her other hand.

The equipment kept beeping in a steady rhythm as the two children watched.

"We're happy you're home, Mom. I wish Daddy was here too."

There was an almost indistinguishable flicker of Kirsten's eyelids.

"She squeezed my hand." Sean raised the volume of his voice.

"Mine too." Kelly started to cry again.

Then there was nothing. The nurse came to the door.

"My mom squeezed our hands!" Sean couldn't keep the excitement inside.

The nurse checked the readouts on the machinery then told the children they had one more minute before they would have to leave.

Kelly leaned over and gave her mother's hand a kiss. "I love you, Mom. Please wake up soon."

Sean watched Kelly then kissed his mother's other hand and repeated Kelly's words. There was no further response. They all left then and walked back to the waiting room where Margaret sat reading.

Chapter Forty-five

A couple of hours of short visitations passed before a doctor came by to check on her. He came in to the waiting room to tell all of her visitors that she was going to be prepped for surgery once again to remove the bone fragment from her spine. It was imperative that it be removed. Apparently, one of the neurosurgeons plus a staff neurologist had gone over all the reports, x-rays, a previous MRI and the one taken in this hospital and was quite certain it could successfully be done.

It was suggested they return home and wait to hear from the doctor, which probably would not be until early in the morning. The children asked if they could just give her one more kiss before they left. He agreed so they shuffled into her room together, each kissing a hand and telling her they'd be back the next day.

"Why don't we eat supper out? We can go to Swiss Chalet just like we did when Maggie arrived in Hamilton."

The children stopped dead in their tracks. "Grandpa, you remembered!" Kelly's eyes were dancing.

Clarke laughed and winked at Margaret. "Yes, I did."

"Does that mean your brain is all healed?" Sean took his grandfather's hand.

"I guess it does. Maggie wants me to make an appointment with the doctor just to make sure, but I think *she* wants to make sure I know what I'm saying when I tell her I love her."

"Grandpa, you do love her. You told us she's your girlfriend." Sean looked at Clarke and said, "You're just teasing us. You know you love her."

They drove to a Swiss Chalet and ordered their dinners.

"What would you kids say if I told you that I don't want Maggie to be my girlfriend any longer."

Three horrified sets of eyes turned to him.

"Well, I don't." He looked from one to the other. "I want her to be my wife."

The last was said as turned to look Margaret directly in the eye.

"You mean she'll really be our grandmother then?" Kelly was smiling from ear to ear.

"You betcha."

"Grandma, please say yes. We want you to be his wife. Please, please." There was a begging tone to Sean's voice.

Margaret placed her napkin beside her plate. "I already said yes."

"Can I be your flower girl?"

"Kelly, that's being a little forward. You're putting Maggie on the spot. We haven't even made any plans about when or where."

"I told your grandfather I wouldn't marry him until his brain was healthy." She had a hard time keeping a serious tone to her voice. "Now that he knows what he's saying, I think as soon as your mother wakes up and gives us her blessing, we can start making plans."

"But, Maggie, I thought —"

"Don't you think your daughter might be disappointed to wake up and realize she missed her own father's wedding?"

She could almost see the thoughts running through Clarke's head.

"But, Grandma, does that mean you will be moving out again?"

Clarke turned to look from Kelly to Margaret. "Yes, Grandma, is that what you mean?"

Sean took a stance. "Grandma, we don't want you to leave. Besides your house is being reno … reno … renonated. You said it's not healthy to live in all that dust and everything."

"Yes, Grandma." Clarke had a mischievous twinkle in his eye. "We don't want your lungs to be contaminated."

"You should be ashamed of yourself, talking like this in front of your grandchildren. We'll discuss it later."

"Nothing to discuss. At least until your *renonations* are completed you have to stay with us, if only for your health. That's final." He winked at her.

She took hold of Clarke's hand under the table.

"Does this mean you are engaged?" Kelly's eyes were shining.

"Yes, Kelly, I guess it does."

"Then you have to give Grandma an engagement ring."

"An engagement ring? What's that?"

"Sean, you don't know anything. It's a ring with a huge diamond on it that a man gives his girlfriend when he asks her to marry him."

Margaret couldn't hold back a slight laugh. "It doesn't have to be a huge diamond. It doesn't have to be a diamond at all. In fact, many couples get married without engagement rings. They just exchange gold bands at the wedding."

"That's not what our babysitter told us. She said that when she gets engaged her boyfriend better give her the biggest diamond ring he can find. That way she'll know he really wants her. You really want Grandma, don't you Grandpa?"

"Yes. I really want her. I really love her. I won't embarrass her by not giving her an engagement ring that way all her friends will know how much I want her." He was laughing too at this point.

Margaret could have hugged the children for inadvertently making him laugh after weeks and weeks of his not being able to even smile. She looked at Kelly, "I think when we get around to it, our wedding will be small so I won't need a flower girl." She saw Kelly's lip quiver. "But we may have a small party and I would need you to help look after the guest book."

"Really?" The girl's face lit up. "How would I do that?"

"Well, you would have to go shopping with me to pick one out, then when the guests arrive you would sit at a table with a nice pen, maybe with a white feather decorating it and you would welcome everyone and make sure they all sign the book so we have a permanent record of who was there to share the occasion."

"What can I do?" Sean wasn't about to be left out.

"Oh, I have a very special job for you, Sean."

"What, Grandpa?"

"It's a secret. It's man stuff so we can't talk about it in front of the ladies." He winked at Sean.

"Wow. See, Kell? I get to do man's stuff." His face lit up with a grin.

Clarke and Margaret watched the joy in the children's faces and almost as if on cue, they turned in unison and kissed each other soundly.

❣ ❣ ❣

After the children had said their prayers and asked God to deliver their mother safely through the surgery, they went to bed with happy thoughts about a wedding which offset, in a way, the fear they were experiencing about their mother's surgery.

"Clarke, that worked out so well. I'm glad we were able to take the children's minds off Kirsten for a little while."

"It worked for me too. It's giving me a feeling of hope and joy instead of only fear for my daughter."

"Come and sit with me."

"As much as I hate to admit it, you are right about waiting for Kirsten to know about our engagement before we just up and get married. It was thoughtless of me even to consider it."

"I'm glad you agree. I'll see how much longer the renovations are going to take. I can stay with Olivia."

He put his arm around her shoulder and pulled her close. "Now that I don't agree with."

"Clarke, we can't sleep together with the children in the same house."

"We can and we will. They accept it naturally knowing you've been sleeping in my bed all the time I've been away. They know you can't sleep in your house right now. They never raised an eyebrow or asked a single question when they woke us up in bed this morning."

"But ..."

"But nothing. They are innocent. Someone else might put lewd thoughts in their heads but they won't even think about anything sinful."

"How can you talk like that when you preached the opposite for all those years?"

"I will keep you an honest woman, Margaret."

She felt like a child being chastised when he used her proper name.

"It's not my honesty or good name that I'm concerned about, it's yours. You are an ordained minister and people look to you to set an example."

"I'm not asking you to stay with me out of lust." He looked directly at her. "Although I will look forward to that part of it. I am asking you for the companionship. If I had a spare bedroom, you could sleep there. Ah, Maggie, girl. I need you here. I need the comfort of your body beside me in the night. I need the comfort of you holding my hand, my arm, anything, otherwise I lie thinking of my daughter and what is ahead for her. What's ahead for her children, my grandchildren? What's ahead for her husband, their father? Will life ever be normal for them again?

"God brought us together for a reason and I truly believe that reason is so we're not alone in our old age. For thirty-two years I was alone and was never attracted to any woman. Then in my golden years, you come along and all of a sudden I don't want to be alone anymore. Even for those few weeks that I was having trouble remembering you, I knew you were the one for me. I sensed it. You were special, and I was attracted to you. When I started getting flashes of times with you, I couldn't get enough of them. I prayed for them not to disappear, and finally it happened. Maggie, I can't live without you. Stay with me."

"I'll stay with you until my house is ready."

"We have to talk about where we are going to live after all this craziness dies down. My biggest fear is that Kirsten might come out of this with permanent paralysis and that her husband is never found. For the two of us, we can live either here or in your place but if we end up with the responsibility of the children and my daughter, we have to give serious thought to another place altogether."

"Do you really think there's a chance Kirsten might end up a quadriplegic?"

"There's a chance. Hopefully we'll find out in the morning that's not going to happen. Maybe I'm being premature in my marriage proposal. I probably should have waited until you knew whether you are only getting a husband or if you've won the lottery and getting a lifetime of caregiving and parenting."

"Stop talking like that, Clarke. We'll do whatever is required of us and we'll do it together. If we have to take care of Kirsten for the rest of our lives, then we'll make the decision of where to live at that time. Probably the best thing to do would be to move into a large bungalow here or go back to Hamilton and live in their house. Let's not get ahead of ourselves."

He sat staring straight ahead.

"Come, darling. Let's go to bed." She took his hand and pulled him to his feet.

Chapter Forty-six

He was awake before the sun came up and phoned the hospital from the kitchen. The nurse on duty told him that Kirsten was still in the recovery area but was expected back in ICU within the half hour. The doctor was scheduled to call them after the patient was back in the unit. He passed this information on to Margaret when he saw her standing in the doorway.

"Sorry I woke you up. I tried to be quiet."

"You didn't wake me. I felt you get out of bed and waited to see if you were coming back."

"Come here." He reached for her and drew her close to him. "I don't think I've told you yet today how much I love you." He kissed her gently.

The phone rang and he picked it up after the first ring. "Mr. Ingram, this is Dr. Dahli. I just saw your daughter and she appears to have come through the surgery well. It's going to take some time before she can move but I'm quite certain that with physiotherapy and patience she will recover her mobility. She's weak and needs to rest after this last ordeal. I recommend we let her sleep for a few hours, maybe put off visiting until noon or so. I will check in on her again in an hour or so to make sure she's stable."

He said if Clarke had questions to leave them with the nurse and he would answer them later.

"She survived, is stable and her chances of mobility are good."

"Our prayers have been answered. Oh, Clarke. I am so happy for her, for the children and for you." She hugged him hard.

"I'll let the children sleep — they need it. We'll tell them when they wake up. They've had three hectic, stressful days and I don't care if they miss another day of school. In another hour or so, I'll call Gerald and Helen."

He stared at Margaret for a long time. "You are the best thing that has come into my life since my grandchildren were born. You are a good luck charm."

She burst out laughing. "Listen to you. You had a quiet peaceful life until you met me. Since then you almost died, your daughter almost died and your son-in-law is missing. Do you honestly think I brought you good luck?"

He looked startled then hugged her and started laughing also. "Well, when you put it that way …"

❣ ❣ ❣

The children were jumping up and down at the good news about their mother. Margaret left them all to enjoy breakfast together and went to her place. She had to meet the builder there and go over the remaining renovations and choose her appliances.

Helen dropped in to exchange hugs and invite her to play bridge the following Tuesday. The next two days were rather routine with hospital visits, meeting school buses and preparing meals. On Friday, she opted to go for lunch with her friends and to get her scheduled manicure and pedicure during the afternoon, so Clarke went to the hospital by himself. When she arrived at his place just before supper, the children met her excitedly at the door.

"Grandpa says Mommy looked at him and smiled today." Kelly was tearing up as she spoke. "Isn't that the best news?"

Sean piped up. "He says we can go to visit her tonight. I hope she looks at us too. Grandpa said not to get our hopes up too high in case she's tired and is sleeping."

"That's wonderful news."

"Will you come with us Grandma? If she's awake maybe she'll see you, too."

"Well now, we wouldn't want to tire her out. Maybe I can watch from the doorway."

Clarke kissed her forehead. "Grandma's right. It might confuse her to find out you have a grandma before she's had time to get used to her surroundings. Don't forget, she doesn't know yet that I've asked Maggie to marry me. Let's give her some time."

The children almost ran down the hospital corridor and had a hard time presenting a calm demeanour when they entered Kirsten's room. Margaret watched from the doorway as they each took one of their mother's hands.

Sean leaned over the side of the bed and whispered, "Mom, Mom are you awake?" Margaret saw the patient's eyes open and Sean and Kelly look at each other with eyes like saucers.

Clarke was standing at the foot of the bed and he told the children to kiss their mother. Kirsten received a kiss on each cheek and her eyes went from side to side as a weak smile caused her lips to open and curl slightly. Her lips moved as if trying to form a word but then her eyes closed and the smile faded.

Kelly looked at her grandfather. "Is Mom okay?"

"Yes, she's more than okay but I think that's all she can manage for now. Why don't you sit and quietly take turns telling her about school today?"

Kelly started telling her about having to catch up on some homework they had missed when they were out of school the day before and Sean told her about the bowling league he had joined. They chatted on for about fifteen minutes then Clarke suggested that might be enough for tonight but they could come back the next day, Saturday.

In the car on the way home, Kelly seemed to withdraw once again. Sean was chattering endlessly but Kelly sat and stared out the window. When they got home, Margaret followed Kelly into her room.

"Do you have a question about your mom, Kelly? You were awfully quiet on the way home."

"I just wish my dad could have been there to see my mom open her eyes. I miss him and I'll bet my mother wonders where he is and why he doesn't come to visit. Where do you think he is Grandma?"

"Oh my poor darling. How hard it must be for you wondering and worrying about your dad. I wish I had some answers for you, but no one seems to know what has happened to him. I still pray that he's safe somewhere and have placed my faith in God that he's being cared for."

"Do you think he's dead?"

Oh dear, how should she answer that. "We have no way of knowing. If he is, then I know he is with God because he was a good man and would have been invited into God's home."

"Why can't God let us know that he's with him? I just want to know if he is or he isn't."

"We can pray together if you like."

"Yes, I like it when you pray with me. You help to say words that I wouldn't know how to say by myself. My mother used to pray with me too."

After their conversation with God was done and Margaret leaned over the bed to kiss Kelly good night, the girl pulled her close with a tight hug. "Grandma, I wish you could stay here forever. I hate that you're getting your condo fixed up and that you're going to be moving back to it soon. Sean says so, too. We love you so much."

Margaret blinked back tears. "When your grandpa and I are married, we'll be together all the time and even after your mother is able to leave the hospital, I can stay and help look after all of you. I love you and your brother, too. You are the only grandchildren I have. You get to sleep now and we'll visit your mother again tomorrow."

Chapter Forty-seven

When they arrived at the hospital the next day, they were surprised to see Kirsten lying in bed staring wide-eyed at the ceiling.

"Mom." The children called out in unison.

Their mother didn't move but they could see a smile form on her face. On closer view they all saw the brace keeping her head and neck immobile.

Margaret had stayed back near the door. There were four beds side by side on the far side of the room and Kirsten was in one of those against the right side wall. She was happy to see that the younger woman was awake and seemingly alert. She motioned to Clarke she would wait in the visitor's lounge. It wasn't the time for her presence or for the kids to refer to her as Grandma.

About ten minutes later, Clarke made his way into the room. He was walking with much more determination and steadiness. A smile was pasted on his face.

"She's awake and recognizes us. She even mouthed us kisses but isn't speaking. I just stopped by the desk and the nurse said Kirsten is trying to speak but seems unable to do so. The neurosurgeon hasn't made his rounds yet, but should be here soon, so maybe we'll find out why."

"Did the children seem disappointed that she's not talking to them?"

"They looked alarmed at first, but when I spoke with Kirsten and she responded with a smile or a wink, they seemed okay with that. I'm sure they'll have questions, but for now I suggested they talk to her in a way that she doesn't have to reply."

"It must be such a relief for you to see her bright."

"Yes." He sat in the chair beside hers. "I'm relieved to know that she has the capability to recognize and understand us, but I want to know the extent of the brain injury that's keeping her from talking. I guess we'll learn more over the next couple of days just what the total damage is that was wreaked on her by that accident. I am so damn glad to have her here where we can watch her progress. I think the children will give her the boost she needs to recover."

"Do you think she's wondering about Mitchell?"

"No doubt that would be her first question if she could talk. I'll discuss it with the doctor when he gets here. I think the sooner she knows the situation the better because she may jump to conclusions."

Clarke looked around the small room. There were half a dozen vinyl-covered, chrome-armed chairs, a three-seater sofa to match and a couple of tables with neatly stacked magazines. Two windows provided a brightness that gave the room a bit of cheeriness for visitors who, no doubt, had enough darkness happening in their lives given the area of the hospital they were visiting.

A few minutes later, Sean peeked his head around the door and informed Clarke that the doctor was in his mother's room. Margaret sat for about a half hour before she could hear all three talking as they walked down the hall toward her. Sean started to speak but was interrupted by Kelly. "Let Grandpa explain it to her so she gets it right."

They sat down, with all their attention turned to Clarke.

"Apparently there is some swelling in the brain still. It will eventually go away but in the meantime, it's affecting her speech and some other of her cognitive skills. They will start various forms of therapy once they can determine the exact extent of her injuries. It could take quite a long time. She requires a few more surgeries to repair some of the bone and tissue injuries some of which will be cosmetic, others will be repair work. She will remain here for the next three to four weeks, then after assessment, will probably be moved to a long-term rehabilitation facility. It may be six months or as long as a year, depending on her mobility. The doctors are pleased with her responsiveness. It appears most of the important areas of her brain are functioning normally." He looked at the children. "Needless to say, that's a huge relief to all of us, eh, kids?"

They nodded their responses.

"He suggested we limit our visiting times to an hour in the afternoon and again in the evening. She, the doctors and therapists have a lot of work ahead of them and the majority of it takes place during the day." He looked at the kids again. "Did I miss anything?"

"Just that she blew us kisses." Kelly burst out laughing and crying at the same time.

"Yeah, she blew kisses at us." Sean's response was uncharacteristically subdued.

Clarke asked the kids to stay with Margaret for a minute while he went back to clarify something. When he returned, Margaret caught a slight nod and she decided not to ask any questions. If it was something she should know, he would tell her later.

And he did. The doctor had said to give Kirsten one more day and then she must be told about her missing husband. It would be too devastating for her to learn accidentally. Clarke took the children back to visit again after supper. The next morning, they all went to the church for Sunday service Clarke regularly attended on Kent Street.

Sunday evening, he went up alone to the hospital. He was honest with the children and told them he needed to talk to their mother alone, father to daughter.

"It's going to be hard for her to learn that your dad is missing. He is her husband and she might well become quite emotional. I want her to be able to do that. If you two are there, she may feel she has to put on a brave face in front of you and I don't want to force her to do that. If she wants to cry, I want her to feel free to cry her heart out. I also want her to know there is hope. He's not been found and people are still looking for him and praying for him."

He looked at the sad eyes in front of him. "When you go up to see her tomorrow you can talk about it with her if you like. It might help her to know you are praying for him and hoping he'll be found."

They all followed him down to his parking spot after supper and waved sadly as he backed out and drove away.

"I hope Momma is going to be okay. She'll be so sad." Sean was the last to turn and go back inside to catch the elevator upstairs.

"You don't think the news about my dad will make her really sick again, do you?" Kelly was holding tightly to Margaret's hand.

"I don't think it will be as hard on her with your grandpa being the one to give her the news as it would be if she heard it accidentally from someone else. Your grandpa is smart to do it this way."

She helped them pick out their clothes for school the next day and together they decided on what they would put in their lunch bags in the morning. In the freezer, they still had banana muffins that Sarah had baked for them so those with cheese and fruit would be their breakfast.

Sean was excited because he learned his bowling team would

be starting regular league play on the following weekend. Olivia had taken him shopping and they had bought top-of-the-line bowling shoes. Margaret had chided her on that because the way he was growing she doubted they would still fit him halfway through the season.

It didn't seem very long before Clarke was home again. He said the nurse had been given instructions to give Kirsten a sedative if she needed it after hearing about her missing husband. So he had waited long enough to make sure she was settled before leaving.

"Is she okay, Grandpa?" Sean's voice was barely more than a whisper.

"Yes, I think so. When she can't talk it's hard to tell. I explained the situation to her. I don't know if anyone had ever told her exactly what had happened. I went through the fact that they were on their way home because of my accident. She looked a little worried about that, but I stood up and told her to look at how good I am now and not to worry about me anymore. I explained why she's in the hospital in Ottawa and that's how I worked around to telling her about your dad." He put his arm around the two children. "I explained to her about the police, the embassy and the mission people all working on finding him. I told her that Maggie was here helping me with the two of you."

He took a breath and waited for questions but when there were none, he went on. "She remembers talking with you on the phone, Maggie. She smiled slightly when I asked her about that. I had to blot her eyes a couple of times because she was crying and can't turn her head with that brace on. I haven't told her about our wedding plans yet. I thought she had enough to think about without that. We'll save that for a few more days and tell her all together. It will give her something positive to smile about.

"I held her hand and talked a little about how we got along in Hamilton waiting for them to come home and how big a help

Maggie had been during that time and then how we arrived at the decision to come to Ottawa. The nurse finally came in and told me my visiting time was up. Your mom seemed distressed at me leaving so the nurse put a sedative in her intravenous tube and I waited until she fell asleep."

"Is she gonna be okay, Grandpa?" Kelly asked this time.

"Of course, she is. She's my daughter after all. She comes from good strong stock. It's just going to take time." He gave them each a hug. "Now off to bed with you. I'll come to say good night in a few minutes."

"Is she going to be okay, Clarke?" Margaret slid an arm around his waist as she slid in beside him on the sofa.

"I hope so, Maggie. I really hope so."

Chapter Forty-eight

Two weeks later Kirsten was able to mouth a few barely distinguishable words after having her broken jaw reset and in a brace. She was regaining feeling and slight movement in her hands and arms. She could not move her toes but was showing signs of feeling in them. Everything was positive. She had undergone another surgery to reset a bone in her elbow and then another to remove some gravel debris from one shoulder. A physiotherapist worked with her twice daily and while progress was slow, there were definite signs of improvement.

Sean had brought his bowling shoes to show his mother and Kelly was full of news about placing second in an intramural spelling competition. It was good enough to allow her to move on to the Eastern Ontario division. All of this put a smile on Kirsten's face. Margaret was watching all the interaction from the doorway just out of Kirsten's line of sight. A few minutes later, Clarke cleared his throat and nodded to the children. Their faces lit up and they looked toward Margaret.

"Mom, we have a surprise for you."

Clarke moved toward the door and took Margaret's hand.

"Yeah." Sean was beaming. "We brought Grandpa's girlfriend for you to meet."

"Sean! You spoiled the surprise." Kelly's eyes shot daggers at her brother.

Margaret watched Kirsten's face as she and Clarke came into her line of view.

Kirsten smiled. A nice warm smile and made a talking sound. It sounded like "Maggie", but Margaret couldn't be sure.

"Yes, Kirsten, this is Maggie. I'm happy to finally introduce you to each other."

"I'm pleased to meet you, Kirsten." Margaret smiled warmly at the young woman and squeezed the hand resting on the bed.

"Thank you." Margaret had no difficulty understanding the words.

Kirsten had tears in the eyes she was moving to take in the whole group. "Thank you." She said again.

Margaret got the message. The woman was thanking her for taking care of her family.

"I'm sure you must know by now that I've come to love your children very much. I'm only sorry that your own tragedy is the reason I continue to have the pleasure of their company."

Kirsten blew her a kiss which Margaret returned.

"Hey, what about me?" Clarke broke the moment. "What about the pleasure of her father's company?"

Everyone laughed, and Margaret added, "Yes, Clarke, I love having the pleasure of your company, too."

"Can we tell her now, Grandpa?"

Clarke took Margaret's hand and looking at Kirsten said, "The kids and I have been waiting for you to be well enough for us to give you some news."

Margaret could see by Kirsten's eyes that she knew what was coming.

"I asked Maggie to be my wife and she accepted."

"Yes, and so they're getting married." Sean was anxious for his mother to know exactly what was happening.

Kirsten didn't hesitate. She blew a kiss to both of them. "Happy," she said.

Margaret couldn't hold back the tears. She walked to the side of the bed and reached for Kirsten's hand and squeezed it. "I'm happy you're happy. I was hoping you would give us your blessing."

"Yippee." Sean was spinning around. "Now she's really gonna be our grandma."

"Mom, do you mind if we call her Grandma?" Kelly was hesitant.

Kirsten winked at Kelly. "Happy." Then she looked at her dad. "When?"

"When you are a little stronger."

"Grandma said the wedding will be small so she won't need a flower girl but I can look after the guest book."

Kirsten looked at her own hand and with great effort lifted her thumb into a symbolic thumb's up sign.

"Grandpa, did you forget something?" Sean was tugging on his grandfather's shirt.

All eyes turned to Clarke. He started to laugh. "Since there won't be a need for a flower girl there also won't be a need for a ring bearer. We don't need two people to look after the guest book and Sean's not old enough to be my best man in the sense of being a witness on the marriage certificate, but he is helping me in a very important way."

Sean was almost bursting through his skin with excitement.

"He and I went shopping and he helped me with a purchase. I needed help in choosing something special. Do you have it with you, Sean?"

The little boy dug into his pocket and pulled out a small package. He opened it and handed a small jewellery box to his grandfather. Clarke took it and reached for Margaret's hand. "Kelly said every man has to give his fiancé a big diamond. You said you didn't need a diamond ring so with Sean's help I picked out a ring to commemorate the month you and I met, the month of May." He removed an emerald ring from its case and placed it on her third finger, left hand. Before she could start to cry he kissed her on both cheeks then brushed her lips with his. "I love you, Maggie."

Then she did cry. The kids cheered and when everyone turned to Kirsten she also had tears streaming down her cheeks. They set a tentative date for a month later in the hopes that Kirsten might be able to sit in a wheelchair.

❧ ❧ ❧

After the children were in bed, Margaret and Clarke sat on the balcony and enjoyed a nice crisp autumn evening. Margaret played with the ring on her finger.

"Clarke, you know I didn't need a ring of any kind not just a diamond."

"I know, sweetheart, but I *wanted* to give you a ring. A beautiful ring that might have more meaning than a diamond."

"It was sweet of you to involve Sean in the purchase."

Clarke laughed. "Yes, he was so funny. He really did help me. We had to look at several stores before we found one we could both agree on. He liked the traditional emerald cut and I liked the platinum setting. We both learned a lot about gemstones and he learned how to keep a secret." He giggled and kissed the ring on her finger.

"We have so much to talk about, so many plans to make. When you talked about the possibility of Kirsten sitting in a wheelchair, I had a thought. Why don't we have the ceremony in the chapel at the hospital?"

"That's why I love you so much, Maggie. You are always thinking of everyone else. That's a wonderful idea. Maybe the pastor from my church will perform the ceremony so Kirsten can be present." He thought for a moment. "Maybe we can have wedding cake and pictures there. After that, our friends can join us at the Merciers' condo for our reception. What do you think? Did you have something else in mind?"

"I think that would be perfect. It's just enough to include

Kirsten but not too much to tire her out. I hope she improves enough to sit in a wheelchair."

"We may have to put our honeymoon on hold for a while."

Chapter Forty-nine

"What do you mean you'll put your honeymoon on hold? You'll do no such thing. Not as long as I've got a breath in my body you won't." Olivia looked like she had been stabbed. "If any couple ever deserved a honeymoon it's you two. After all you've been through you need to get away — just the two of you — even if it's only for a few days. The two of you haven't had a single day to spend together in the last several months without someone needing you."

"Well, under the circumstances, we can't. We just can't. That's all there is to it."

The girls had come over to Margaret's condo for an afternoon of bridge. Their games had been suspended for a short time because of her inability to attend. Another neighbour, Stella Jacobson, filled in once in a while when one of them couldn't attend, but she was not always available. The last time Margaret had been available for a game was the day she made the announcement about Clarke coming into her life. That day had been an eternity ago she thought when setting up the table for bridge.

They discussed the wedding plans, Kirsten's recovery, the children's schooling, Clarke's unsuccessful attempts at locating his missing son-in-law and who had moved in and out of the building. Now, it was time to plan the honeymoon or non-honeymoon as it now sat.

"Okay, supposing you and Clarke *could* go away for a honeymoon, what would be your ideal place to go?"

"I was always trying to talk Hugh into going on a European river cruise. I always watch the commercials and think how relaxing they must be, plus the added feature of visiting all those historic cities along the way."

"That's right, you said Hugh was not a traveller. Is Clarke?"

"We've talked about the places we might like to see together, this cruise is one of them, but we both know all travel plans will be on hold until Kirsten is in a suitable long-term care facility and we know what has happened to her husband. We can't just up and leave the children and her."

"Why not?" Sarah was almost curt.

"How would it be if we were over in Europe and Mitchell was found in some prison or cave or God knows where? Or if he showed up in Hamilton and no one was there to help him."

"Margaret, you can't put your life on hold indefinitely. What if the man doesn't want to be found? God forbid, but he could be living the high life somewhere without a care in the world."

"I know that, Helen, but we can wait a year or so. We're only in our early sixties. It's not like we're eighty-five and every year is a gift."

"I'm just saying you and Clarke have been doing so much for his family for months now and it wouldn't hurt to take a week off and enjoy each other. Alone. Together. You know what I mean."

"We will, just not yet." She gathered in the tricks she had won. "Now, who's ready for coffee and dessert? I made the best strudel in my new oven this morning."

They went on to talk about other things until it was time for Margaret to leave. They helped carry the dishes to be loaded into the dishwasher.

"I'll give you girls a shout tomorrow after we've talked to the minister and the doctor. We're just waiting for the official go-ahead before making final plans. Kirsten is coming along really well."

"Is there any movement in her legs yet?"

"No, and her hand/eye coordination is still off, but at least she's able to hold some things in her hands now and with a little effort is able to get a piece of toast from a plate to her mouth. She's building strength in her arms and soon she'll be able to pull herself up off the pillow. She's speaking quite a bit better now after thrice weekly sessions with a speech therapist."

"That's a long way from where she was a couple of weeks ago." Olivia had been in to meet her shortly after their engagement was official.

❣ ❣ ❣

Two days later, they chose their wedding date as the third Friday in October. They decided a week day would work better because full staff was on at the hospital to assist with Kirsten and they were all retired, so they didn't need to have their wedding on a weekend. A day out of school was always welcomed by the children. The pastor from the Presbyterian Church would perform the ceremony. Helen and Gerald were going to be their attendants and Olivia and Sarah would look after the catering for the dozen or so guests. The reception would be at the Merciers' condominium. Kelly was included in the shopping for dresses and flowers and the guest book. Hair appointments were booked. Clarke took Sean to get new pants, dress shoes and a tie. They felt there was no need for him to wear a suit. Both children took several selections to the hospital for their mother's approval. Olivia offered to do Kirsten's hair and makeup that day and also bought her a beautiful long caftan she could slip on easily, and dressy slippers for her feet.

Finally, the day arrived and all was in readiness. Kirsten's wheelchair was placed in the front row. Sean was seated in a chair beside her where Kelly joined them once all the guests had signed the book. Clarke stood to one side at the front with Gerald beside him. Someone had seen to setting up the proper music on the player near the altar. At the proper time, Helen preceded Margaret into the little chapel. Margaret had chosen a simple lilac-coloured dress with three-quarter-length sleeves and a single strand of pearls.

She looked at Clarke in his grey suit and light purple tie. He was the most handsome man alive in that moment. She took his hand. He didn't take his eyes from hers as they repeated their wedding vows and were declared husband and wife. Sean let out a hooray before Kelly could stop him.

A photographer was present and took pictures as they kissed, then a posed portrait as they cut the cake and then several that included Kirsten and the children, then the wedding party and several candid shots of the guests enjoying the cake.

The bride and groom stayed until Kirsten was settled back in her room. She motioned to them to open the drawer in her night stand. There was an envelope containing a beautiful card and inside was a pair of airline tickets to Europe and two tickets for a boat cruise through The Netherlands and Germany. Margaret looked up to see tears in Kirsten's eyes. "I love you both. Now go and join your wedding party and let me sleep."

"But—" Clarke squeezed Margaret's arm before she could get anything else out. When she looked back at Kirsten, the woman had her eyes closed.

"Clarke, we can't accept this gift. How can we get away?"

"We can and we shall. We'll work it out. I know my daughter and that's her way of saying thank you."

"I wonder how she … Never mind, I know how." Margaret remembered the conversation with her friends the last time they had played bridge.

The party was in full swing by the time they arrived. Olivia had gone overboard with food and drink and everyone seemed to be enjoying themselves. Helen had assigned jobs for the children and they were busy taking around plates of goodies and picking up used napkins and plates and taking them to the kitchen. About a half hour later the doorbell rang and Kelly opened it to let Stella Jacobson inside.

Stella looked around and saw Margaret. "I am so sorry I missed the ceremony at the chapel. I just couldn't get away from the office in time."

"That's quite all right, Stella. I'm so glad you were able to come and join in now. Come. I want you to meet my husband."

They started across the room to where Clarke was standing with his back to them while in conversation with one of his friends.

"Clarke, I want you to meet another friend and neighbour of mine, Stella Jacobson."

He turned and Stella gasped. "You're … you're married to Pastor Ingram?"

"Yes, do you know each other?"

Clarke took Stella into his arms and gave her a warm hug. "My dear, Stella. It's so nice to see you again."

Stella was crying. "Excuse me. I shouldn't be crying like this at such a happy occasion."

She looked embarrassed and seemed to be struggling to keep her composure.

"Margaret, I didn't know your Clarke was Pastor Ingram. I never put the names together. In fact, I don't think I ever knew your first name." She looked at Clarke.

Margaret didn't know how to respond. Clarke had never mentioned knowing Stella. Maybe Stella's name had never come up.

"Margaret, your husband is truly one of God's disciples sent from heaven above. He is the only one that ever made my son feel like he was worth the space he filled. The Pastor gave my son such happiness even if only for a little while and I know because of him there's a faint hope Jeremy may have squeezed through the doors of heaven."

She gave Margaret a tight bear hug. "You are so blest to have this fine man as your husband. I am so happy you invited me to come and share your wedding celebrations." She turned to Clarke again. "I will pray every day for your happiness."

"Would you like something to eat?" Sean held a plate of smoked salmon and crackers up to Stella. "I'll get my sister to bring you the guest book to sign."

"Who are you, young man?" Stella took some food from the plate.

"That's my grandpa." He pointed to Clarke.

Stella's smile faded. She looked again from Margaret to Clarke. "Of course. It's Pastor Ingram's children you were looking after while he was away with his daughter. I am so sorry." She turned to Clarke. "How is your daughter now?"

"She's coming along, thank you. In fact, she was in the chapel for the wedding — in a wheelchair but there just the same."

"I'm so glad to hear that. If there is ever anything I can do for either of you, please don't hesitate to ask." She left them to get something to drink.

"That poor woman has not had an easy life. The loss of her son was almost the end of her." He shook his head.

Margaret felt even worse for ever having thought badly of Stella Jacobson and even worse for making Stella's life more difficult than it already was.

Chapter Fifty

Kirsten was transferred to a long-term rehabilitation centre. She was making slow but steady progress. There was nothing new on the whereabouts of her husband. Every road led to a dead end. She and the children came to accept that they may never see him again. The hardest part Kirsten had told Margaret was in the not knowing. It would be easier if she knew he was dead than wondering daily as to his well-being. He had been missing for two and a half months and it was difficult to believe he could be alive and not seen for that long.

It was at suppertime three days before their cruise when Margaret answered the ringing phone.

"It's Stella Jacobson, Margaret. I guess you must be busy packing and getting ready for your honeymoon."

"Yes, we're quite excited."

"I won't keep you. I just learned that one of those nice three-bedroom-plus-den condos on the second floor in our building is coming available. Olivia mentioned that you and Clarke were putting off making a decision about finding more suitable living space until after you came back from you trip. I thought of you when I heard about this one."

Margaret hesitated. She had been in one of those larger condos visiting once and had fallen in love with it. She didn't need all that space, nor could she have afforded it, but now the space might be welcome. "Do you know what the selling price is?"

"No, I don't but I can't imagine it would be more than the

combined value of both of your current condos. Connie, in the real estate office on the corner, is handling the sale, if you're interested."

"We might be, Stella. I'll mention it to Clarke but I'm not sure we'll have time to act on it before we leave. Thank you so much for letting us know."

They broke the connection and she told Clarke about the pending vacancy. They agreed it might be worth setting up an appointment to view it before their honeymoon. Three full bedrooms plus a den was certainly an enticement, especially if there was a chance that Kirsten might be allowed an overnight visit once in a while.

❣ ❣ ❣

Clarke and Margaret prepared for their cruise. They were able to book on the last cruise of the season. They were assured the weather in central Europe was still warm enough to enjoy the sights and the water. He had received a clean bill of health from his family physician and she had never been healthier. She smiled every time she thought about her friends being right. All she had needed was a man in her life. She had been fortunate enough to have not just any man come along, but the best man on earth. Superman.

Sarah was going to move in to Clarke's condo for the ten days they would be away. Sean and Kelly were looking forward to the anticipated gourmet meals. Olivia had booked an overnight visit for her and the children in Montreal where they would spend the two-day weekend in the middle of their grandparents' vacation.

The children weren't even crying as they waved their goodbyes at the airport. As she looked back at them, Margaret thought she and Clarke had been so foolish to think the children would miss them. "I think they're almost happy to see us go."

"Of course they are. Sarah and Olivia will spoil them rotten while we're gone."

"They have certainly been resilient with all that has happened to them in the last six months. They've adapted to a totally different life style with only minor complaints."

"You forget who their grandfather is — Superman."

Margaret poked him. "You've really let that go to your head."

They had arranged for wheelchair assistance for Clarke throughout their journey. It would make it much easier for both of them, and certainly more enjoyable for him. They had just boarded the cruise ship in Amsterdam when Clarke's cell phone buzzed.

"Clarke, this is Sarah. I'm so sorry to bother you but I just received a call from the Canadian Embassy in Peru. They wouldn't tell me what it's about other than it's urgent. I thought you would want to know."

When Clarke got through to the name and number Sarah gave him, he was told that Mitchell Sennett might have been found and that he was alive. They were verifying the identification.

"That's wonderful news! How soon will they know if it's Mitchell?"

"The woman didn't say, only that they were working on it. I don't know what they're looking for. I assume he didn't have any identification with him. She really didn't know very much other than the vague information their office had received from somewhere in one of the provinces."

"What do you want to do?"

"I want to have a honeymoon with my wife." He kissed her forehead and suggested they remain aboard until they received any other news. He had given the embassy instructions to call his cell phone if anything further developed. They sent Sarah a text telling her not to mention the call to anyone because of its ambiguity and that it probably shouldn't have been placed until something more definite was available.

The next day, they toured the windmills in Kinderdijk in The Netherlands. Margaret kissed Clarke constantly just for the mere fact he was taking as much pleasure in this travel adventure as she was. "People are going to think we're on our honeymoon or something, the way you can't keep your hands off me."

"I will shout it to the world so there will be no doubt about it. I can't tell you how happy I am." Then she kissed him again.

Two days later, after a day in Cologne, they were just about to sit down for dinner aboard ship when another phone call came through. Mitchell Sennett had been identified and was anxious to return home.

Margaret and Clarke cancelled the remainder of their journey and arranged airline connections for a flight home.

Chapter Fifty-one

Clarke was exhausted when they arrived at the Ottawa airport. Margaret was disappointed about cancelling the balance of their trip, but she knew they had to get back to the children and Kirsten.

Sarah had said nothing to anyone, not even Kirsten. Clarke wanted to talk to Kirsten and the children himself. By the end of the next day, it had been verified that Mitchell was indeed who he said he was. Arrangements were being made to fly him to Ottawa.

It was a long, involved story of mistaken identity. Drug smugglers had killed the American in error thinking he was the useless Canadian. The American had fingered Mitchell as the man they were looking for not realizing he had signed his own death warrant. Mitchell had been held captive and repeatedly tortured all these months by drug merchants who accused him of stealing several millions of dollars in drugs. They kept him alive only because he was no good to them dead. As long as he could breathe and talk, they had a chance of getting information about either the money or the drugs from him.

It was more than a week earlier that a police surveillance drone had caught him in its camera and someone recognized him as possibly the missing Canadian. It took several days to organize a raiding party before they could make any attempt to get him out. Finally, their men were in place and they stormed the compound. Mitchell was first taken to a military hospital and then to Lima.

Clarke and Margaret sat in the office of the Peruvian Embassy in Ottawa. The officials there had done everything that could be expected of them to bring Mitchell back safely. He was thin, emaciated almost, but alert and in seemingly good health. When he saw Clarke, he yelped then started to cry.

"I've been told that my wife is in hospital here. Where is she? How is she?"

"The bus rollover took a real toll on her but fortunately she survived and has been knit back together. With a lot of rehabilitation, love and time she'll hopefully be as good as new one day soon."

"The children?"

"They're living with Margaret and me. They haven't stopped praying for your safe return. None of us has."

"Can I see Kirsten and the kids?"

"A friend of ours is picking them up from school and will meet us at the hospital where Kirsten is."

"She's still in hospital?"

"It's a long-term rehab centre and she'll be there for a while yet. Maybe you being back will be the miracle that will speed her healing. Let's get you over there before the press gets wind of you being here. You may lose some of your privacy once they find out you've been found and returned to Canada."

Clarke filled Mitchell in on everything that transpired during the time he was missing, including his marriage to Margaret and the care she had undertaken of his whole family. Mitchell couldn't help the tears that filled his eyes. When they arrived at the hospital, Clarke suggested he go in first and prepare Kirsten for a surprise visitor.

"Who is it? A new doctor?" All Clarke had told Kirsten was that he had a surprise visitor waiting to come in and that she should comb her hair.

A moment later, Mitchell came through the door, followed

by Margaret. It was a good five minutes before the two loosened their grip on each other. Margaret and Clarke left the room to give them private time together. The elevator doors opened and two concerned-looking children stepped into the hallway.

"What's going on? Is something the matter with Mom?" Sean was on the verge of tears.

"I tried to tell him it was a good surprise but he wouldn't listen." Olivia was right behind the children.

"What's the surprise, Grandpa?" Kelly's look wasn't different from her brother's.

"It's one you're going to like. Let's go see your mom. That's where the surprise is."

They approached the doorway to Kirsten's room and Sean ran through ahead of them. "Mom, Grandpa says you have a surprise for — Dad! Kelly, look. It's Dad." He ran into his father's waiting arms.

Kelly hung back momentarily then covered her face with her hands. "Kelly, come and let me give you a hug." She walked to her dad with her hands still covering her face.

"What's the matter? Why won't you look at me?"

"Because I'm afraid you will disappear if I do — like in a dream."

Mitchell knelt and drew her into his arms. "I'm not going to disappear. I'm going to stay with you forever."

Kirsten suggested that Margaret and Clarke go home and get some rest while she and her family visit. Clarke gave Mitchell money to call Uber to take them home to the apartment when they were ready. Olivia had left after dropping the kids off. Clarke took Margaret's hand as they walked out together.

Mitchell and his son slept in Kelly's room that night and Kelly took her brother's single bed. Everyone was exhausted and consequently slept in the next morning. It was the ringing of the phone that finally woke Clarke up. It was one of the local news people. Someone from the hospital had leaked the story. The rest of the morning was spent answering calls and trying put off interviews at least for a day.

After a few hectic days of seemingly unending, repetitious questions by various media, they finally found some time to discuss what the future might be. Mitchell agreed that Kirsten was getting excellent care and taking the children out of school to be registered again in Hamilton would only be another upheaval for them. His company was willing to give him an extended leave to recuperate and to establish some plans for his family.

"Before Maggie and I left on our trip we placed an offer on a large condominium which had come on the market in her old building. It's just a few blocks from here on Windsor Street. It is large enough to accommodate all of us. You're welcome to stay with us for as long as it takes. Even until school is out if Kirsten's rehabilitation takes that long."

"But you won't need one that large after we're back in Hamilton."

"It will be nice to always have room for family when you want to visit."

Mitchell looked from one to the other. "Why do I have the feeling it's already a done deal?"

"Because it is."

Clarke and Margaret took possession of their new condominium two weeks before Christmas. Their two condos were in the right price range to spark a bidding war and had sold immediately. The bedroom furniture from both places came with them but the new den was furnished with only a single bed and dresser for Mitchell. The rest of the space was left vacant to accommodate a hospital bed and some gym equipment so Kirsten could join them for the week the children would be home over Christmas.

Kirsten was able to get around in a wheelchair by then and remarked how nice it was that their home in Hamilton was already wheelchair accessible. The neurosurgeon had not given her much hope of gaining full use of her legs again, but she and her physiotherapist had other ideas. It was truly a Christmas present of some magnitude when they all slept under the same roof on Christmas Eve.

Everyone sat around the huge dining room table for a traditional turkey dinner the next day. Helen and Gerald joined them as did Sarah and Stella. Olivia, as was her custom, had left to spend six weeks in Florida with friends. All the women had contributed something toward the feast. Even Kirsten had been included. She and Kelly were responsible for the table centre-piece. They worked all morning on setting up a unique display using Margaret's crystal, candles, small evergreen branches and coloured Christmas beads.

When everyone had eaten their fill, the table was cleared and leftovers were packaged for sharing and some for the freezer. After their guests had left, Kirsten and Mitchell sat and read Christmas stories with the children. Clarke and Margaret slipped out to the balcony to look at the bright lights of the city glistening red and green.

"I promise we'll have a proper honeymoon in the New Year, Maggie. Have you ever been to Australia?"

"Australia? No. What is it about Australia that catches your fancy?"

"It's summer down there right now."

"Hmm. That's a long flight for you. Why don't we try going as far as Hawaii first? I'd love to try para-sailing and watching the sunset over the ocean from a hotel balcony or a beach hut."

She snuggled into him with her back against his chest.

"Speaking of views from a balcony, did you notice we can see the Christmas lights on the parliament buildings over there?"

"Another nice thing about living here."

"What's the other thing?"

"I never did have to change my Windsor Street address, just the apartment number."

"I had to change mine."

"That's only fair. I changed my name."

"Yes you did." He slid his arms around her and nibbled her ear. "How about a little kiss, Mrs. Margaret Ingram of 73 Windsor Street?"

Acknowledgements

Many thanks to my talented book designer, friend and critic, Sherrill Wark at Crowe Creations; to the members of the Bells Corners Writing Circle who continue to keep me on my game and to my family who always inspire and support me.

About the Author

Phyllis always knew her destiny was to be a writer. It took retirement and a few decades of working with numbers before she reached it. Now she's doing what she loves to do most — writing to her heart's content balanced with a great deal of reading. She and her husband live quietly in the Ottawa area close to their three adult children, a few grandchildren and one great-grandchild.

Margaret McFarland is the second novel in the *72 Windsor* series. Watch for the third book sometime in 2019. Besides these two, Phyllis has four Romantic/Suspense novels published and is currently working on another.

As a change of pace, she has written several children's puppet plays that are performed daily, in season, at The Valleyview Little Animal Farm in Richmond, Ontario.

A complete listing of her work can be found on her website: www.phyllisbohonis.com

Also by Phyllis Bohonis

ROMANCE
Tomorrow's Promise

ROMANTIC SUSPENSE
Fire in the Foothills
The Wilderness
The Track

73 WINDSOR SERIES
Helen Whittaker

CPSIA information can be obtained
at www.ICGtesting.com
Printed in the USA
LVHW08s0849160818
586894LV00003B/5/P